Prince Hagen

Upton Sinclair

Contents

ACT I 7

ACT II 33

ACT III 57

ACT IV 80

PRINCE HAGEN

BY

Upton Sinclair

ACT I

SCENE I

[Shows a primeval forest, with great trees, thickets in background, and moss and ferns underfoot. A set in the foreground. To the left is a tent, about ten feet square, with a fly. The front and sides are rolled up, showing a rubber blanket spread, with bedding upon it; a rough stand, with books and some canned goods, a rifle, a fishing-rod, etc. Toward centre is a trench with the remains of a fire smoldering in it, and a frying pan and some soiled dishes beside it. There is a log, used as a seat, and near it are several books, a bound volume of music lying open, and a violin case with violin. To the right is a rocky wall, with a cleft suggesting a grotto.]

[At rise: GERALD pottering about his fire, which is burning badly, mainly because he is giving most of his attention to a bound volume of music which he has open. He is a young man of twenty-two, with wavy auburn hair; wears old corduroy trousers and a grey flannel shirt, open at the throat. He stirs the fire, then takes violin and plays the Nibelung theme with gusto.]

GERALD. A plague on that fire! I think I'll make my supper on prunes and crackers to-night!

[Plays again.]

MIMI. [Enters left, disguised as a pack-peddler; a little wizened up man, with long, unkempt grey hair and beard, and a heavy bundle on his back.] Good evening, sir!

GERALD. [Starts.] Hello!

MIMI. Good evening!

GERALD. Why... who are you?

MIMI. Can you tell me how I find the road, sir?

GERALD. Where do you want to go?

MIMI. To the railroad.

GERALD. Oh, I see! You got lost?

MIMI. Yes, sir.

GERALD. [Points.] You should have turned to the right down where the roads cross.

MIMI. Oh. That's it!

[Puts down burden and sighs.]

GERALD. Are you expecting to get to the railroad to-night?

MIMI. Yes, sir.

GERALD. Humph! You'll find it hard going. Better rest. [Looks him over, curiously.] What are you--a peddler?

MIMI. I sell things. Nice things, sir. You buy?

[Starts to open pack.]

GERALD. No. I don't want anything.

MIMI. [Gazing about.] You live here all alone?

GERALD. Yes... all alone.

MIMI. [Looking of left.] Who lives in the big house?

GERALD. That's my father's camp.

MIMI. Humph! Nobody in there?

GERALD. The family hasn't come up yet.

MIMI. Why don't you live there?

GERALD. I'm camping out--I prefer the tent.

MIMI. Humph! Who's your father?

GERALD. John Isman's his name.

MIMI. Rich man, hey?

GERALD. Why... yes. Fairly so.

MIMI. I see people here last year.

GERALD. Oh! You've been here before?

MIMI. Yes. I been here. I see young lady. Very beautiful!

GERALD. That's my sister, I guess.

MIMI. Your sister. What you call her?

GERALD. Her name's Estelle.

MIMI. Estelle! And what's your name?

GERALD. I'm Gerald Isman.

MIMI. Humph! [Looking about, sees violin.] You play music, hey?

GERALD. Yes.

MIMI. You play so very bad?

GERALD. [Laughs.] Why... what makes you think that?

MIMI. You come 'way off by yourself!

GERALD. Oh! I see! No... I like to be alone.

MIMI. I hear you playing... nice tune.

GERALD. Yes. You like music?

MIMI. Sometimes. You play little quick tune... so?

[Hums.]

GERALD. [Plays Nibelung theme.] This?

MIMI. [Eagerly.] Yes. Where you learn that?

GERALD. That's the Nibelung music.

MIMI. Nibelung music! Where you hear it?

GERALD. Why... it's in an opera.

MIMI. An opera?

GERALD. It's by a composer named Wagner.

MIMI. Where he hear it?

GERALD. [Laughs.] Why... I guess he made it up.

MIMI. What's it about? Hey?

GERALD. It's about the Nibelungs.

MIMI. Nibelungs?

GERALD. Queer little people who live down inside the earth, and spend all their time digging for gold.

MIMI. Ha! You believe in such people?

GERALD. [Amused.] Why... I don't know...

MIMI. You ever see them?

GERALD. No... but the poets tell us they exist.

MIMI. The poets, hey? What they tell you about them?

GERALD. Well, they have great rocky caverns, down in the depths of the earth. And they have treasures of gold... whole caves of it. And they're very cunning smiths... they make all sorts of beautiful golden vessels and trinkets.

MIMI. Trinkets, hey! [Reaches into bundle.] Like this, hey?

[Holds up a gold cup.]

GERALD. [Surprised.] Oh!

MIMI. Or this, hey?

GERALD. Why... where did you get such things?

MIMI. Ha, ha! You don't know what I got!

GERALD. Let me see them.

MIMI. You think the Nibelungs can beat that, hey? [Reaches into bag.] Maybe I sell you this cap! [Takes out a little cap of woven gold chains.] A magic cap, hey?

GERALD. [Astounded.] Why... what is it?

MIMI. [Puts it on his head.] You wear it... so. And you play Nibelung

music, and you vanish from sight... nobody finds you. Or I sell you
the magic ring... you wear that... [Hands it to GERALD.] Put it on your
finger... so. Now you play, and the Nibelungs come... they dance about
in the woods... they bring you gold treasures... ha, ha, ha! [Amused
at GERALD's perplexity.] What you think they look like, hey?... those
Nibelungs!

GERALD. Why... I don't know...

MIMI. What do your poets tell you? ha?

GERALD. Why... they're little men... with long hair and funny clothes...
and humpbacked.

MIMI. Look like me, hey?

GERALD. [Embarrassed.] Why... yes... in a way.

MIMI. What are their names?

GERALD. Their names?

MIMI. Yes... what ones do you know about?

GERALD. Well, there was Alberich, the king.

MIMI. Alberich!

GERALD. He was the one who found the Rheingold. And then there was
Hagen, his son.

MIMI. Hagen!

GERALD. He killed the hero, Siegfried.

MIMI. Yes, yes!

GERALD. And then there was Mimi.

MIMI. Ah! Mimi!

GERALD. He was a very famous smith.

MIMI. [Eagerly.] You know all about them! Somebody has been there!

GERALD. What do you mean?

MIMI. Would you like to see those Nibelungs?

GERALD. [Laughing.] Why... I wouldn't mind.

MIMI. You would like to see them dancing in the moonlight, and hear the clatter of their trinkets and shields? You would like to meet old King Alberich, and Mimi the smith? You would like to see that cavern yawn open... [points to right] and fire and steam break forth, and all the Nibelungs come running out? Would you like that? ha?

GERALD. Indeed I would!

MIMI. You wouldn't be afraid?

GERALD. No, I don't think so.

MIMI. But are you sure?

GERALD. Yes... sure!

MIMI. All right! You wear my magic ring! You wait till night comes! Then you play! [Puts away trinkets.] I must go now.

GERALD. [Perplexed.] What do you want for your ring?

MIMI. It is not for sale. I give it.

GERALD. What!

MIMI. Money could not buy it. [Takes up pack.] I came to you because you play that music.

GERALD. But I can't... it...

MIMI. It is yours... you are a poet! [Starts left.] Is this the way?

GERALD. Yes. But I don't like to...

MIMI. Keep it! You will see! Good-bye!

GERALD. But wait!

MIMI. It is late. I must go. Good-night.

[Exit left.]

GERALD. Good-night. [Stands staring.] Well, I'll be switched! If that wasn't a queer old customer! [Looks at ring.] It feels like real gold! [Peers after MIMI.] What in the world did he mean, anyhow? The magic ring! I hope he doesn't get lost in those woods to-night. [Turns to fire.] Confound that fire! It's out for good now! Let it go. [Sits, and takes music score.] Nibelungs! They are realer than anybody guesses.

People who spend their lives in digging for gold, and know and care about nothing else. How many of them I've met at mother's dinner parties! Well, I must get to my work now. [Makes a few notes; then looks up and stretches.] Ah, me! I don't know what makes me so lazy this evening. This strange heaviness! There seems to be a spell on me. [Gazes about.] How beautiful these woods are at sunset! If I were a Nibelung, I'd come here for certain! [Settles himself, reclining; shadows begin to fall; music from orchestra.] I'm good for nothing but dreaming... I wish Estelle were here to sing to me! How magical the twilight is! Estelle! Estelle!

[He lies motionless; music dies away, and there is a long silence. The forest is dark, with gleams of moonlight. Suddenly there is a faint note of music... the Nibelung theme. After a silence it is repeated; then again. Several instruments take it up. It swells louder. Vague forms are seen flitting here and there. Shadows move.]

GERALD. [Starting up suddenly.] What's that? [Silence; then the note is heard again, very faint. He starts. It is heard again, and he springs to his feet.] What's that? [Again and again. He runs to his violin, picks it up, and stares at it. Still the notes are heard, and he puts down the violin, and runs down stage, listening.] Why, what can it mean? [As the music grows louder his perplexity and alarm increase. Suddenly he sees a figure stealing through the shadows, and he springs back, aghast.] Why, it's a Nibelung! [Another figure passes.] Oh! I must be dreaming! [Several more appear.] Nibelungs! Why, it's absurd! Wake up, man! You're going crazy! [Music swells louder; figures appear, carrying gold shields, chains, etc., with clatter.] My God!

[He stands with hands clasped to his forehead, while the uproar swells louder and louder, and the forms become more numerous. He rushes down stage, and the Nibelungs surround him, dancing about him in wild career, laughing, screaming, jeering. They begin to pinch his legs behind his back, and he leaps here and there, crying out. Gradually they drive him toward the grotto, which opens before them, revealing a black chasm, emitting clouds of steam. They rush in and are enveloped in the mist. Sounds of falling and crashing are heard. The steam spreads, gradually veiling the front of the stage.]

[Nets rise with the steam, giving the effect of a descent. During this change the orchestra plays the music between Scenes II and III in Das Rheingold.]

SCENE II

[Nibelheim: a vast rocky cavern. Right centre is a large gold throne, and to the right of that an entrance through a great tunnel. Entrances from the sides also. At the left is a large golden vase upon a stand, and near it lie piles of golden utensils, shields, etc. Left centre is a heavy iron door, opening into a vault. Throughout this scene there is a suggestion of music, rising into full orchestra at significant moments. The voices of the Nibelungs are accompanied by stopped trumpets and other weird sounds.]

[At rise: The stage is dark. A faint light spreads. A company of Nibelungs crosses from right to left, carrying trinkets and treasures. Clatter of shields, crack of whips, music, etc. Another company of Nibelungs runs in left.]

FIRST NIB. [Entering.] The earth-man has come!

SECOND NIB. Where is he?

FIRST NIB. He is with Mimi!

SECOND NIB. What is he like?

FIRST NIB. He is big! [With a gesture of fright.] Terrible!

THIRD NIB. Ah!

SECOND NIB. And the king? Does he know?

FIRST NIB. He has been told.

THIRD NIB. Where is the king?

FIRST NIB. He comes! He comes!

[The orchestra plays the Fasolt and Fafnir music, Rheingold, Scene II.]

[Enter a company of Nibelungs, armed with whips, and marching with a stately tread. They post themselves about the apartment. Enter another company supporting KING ALBERICH. He is grey-haired and very feeble, but ferocious-looking, and somewhat taller than the others. His robe is lined with ermine, and he carries a gold Nibelung whip--a short handle of gold, with leather thongs. He seats himself upon the throne, and all make obeisance. A solemn pause.]

ALBERICH. The earth-man has come?

FIRST NIB. Yes, your majesty!

ALB. Where is Mimi?

ALL. Mimi! Mimi!

[The call is repeated off.]

MIMI. [Enters left.] Your majesty.

ALB. Where is the earth-man?

MIMI. He is safe, your majesty.

ALB. Did he resist?

MIMI. I have brought him, your majesty.

ALB. And Prince Hagen? Has he come?

MIMI. He is without, your majesty.

ALB. Let him be brought in.

[All cry out in terror.]

MIMI. Your majesty. He is wild! He fights with everyone! He...

ALB. Let him be brought in.

ALL. Prince Hagen! Prince Hagen!

MIMI. [Calling.] Prince Hagen!

[Some run out. The call is heard off All stand waiting in tense expectation. The music plays the Hagen motives, with suggestions of the Siegfried funeral march. Voices are heard in the distance, and at the climax of the music PRINCE HAGEN and his keepers enter. He is small for a man, but larger than any of the Nibelungs; a grim, sinister figure, with black hair, and a glowering look. His hands are chained in front of him, and eight Nibelungs march as a guard. He has bare arms and limbs, and a rough black bearskin flung over his shoulders. He enters right, and stands glaring from one to another.]

ALB. Good evening, Hagen.

HAGEN. [After a pause.] Well?

ALB. [Hesitating.] Hagen, you are still angry and rebellious?

HAGEN. I am!

ALB. [Pleading.] Hagen, you are my grandson. You are my sole heir... the only representative of my line. You are all that I have in the world!

HAGEN. Well?

ALB. You place me in such a trying position! Have you no shame... no conscience? Why, some day you will be king... and one cannot keep a king in chains!

HAGEN. I do not want to be in chains!

ALB. But, Hagen, your conduct is such... what can I do? You have robbed... you have threatened murder! And you... my grandson and my heir...

HAGEN. Have you sent for me to preach at me again?

ALB. Hagen, this stranger... he has come to visit us from the world above. These earth-men know more than we... they have greater powers...

[He hesitates.]

HAGEN. What is all that to me?

ALB. You know that you yourself are three-quarters an earth-man...

HAGEN. I know it. [With a passionate gesture.] But I am in chains!

ALB. There may be a way of your having another chance. Perhaps this stranger will teach you. If you will promise to obey him, he will stay with you... he will be your tutor, and show you the ways of the earth-men.

HAGEN. No!

ALB. What?

HAGEN. I will not have it!

ALB. Hagen!

HAGEN. I will not have it, I say! Why did you not consult me?

ALB. But what is your objection...

HAGEN. I will not obey an earth-man! I will not obey anyone!

ALB. But he will teach you...

HAGEN. I do not want to be taught. I want to be let alone! Take off these chains!

ALB. [Half rising.] Hagen! I insist...

HAGEN. Take them off, I say! You cannot conquer me... you cannot trick me!

ALB. [Angrily.] Take him away!

[The Nibelungs seize hold of him to hustle him off.]

HAGEN. I will not obey him! Mark what I say... I will kill him. Yes! I will kill him!

[He is dragged off protesting.]

ALB. [Sits, his head bowed with grief, until the uproar dies away; then, looking up.] Mimi!

MIMI. Yes, your majesty.

ALB. Let the earth-man be brought.

MIMI. Yes, your majesty!

ALL. The earth-man! The earth-man!

[The call is heard as before. GERALD is brought on; the orchestra plays a beautiful melody, violins and horns. MIMI moves left to meet him.]

GERALD. [Enters left with attendants; hesitating, gazing about in wonder. He sees MIMI, and stops; a pause.] The pack peddler!

MIMI. The pack peddler!

GER. And these are Nibelungs?

MIMI. You call us that.

GER. [Laughing nervously.] You... er... it's a little disconcerting, you know. I had no idea you existed. May I ask your name?

MIMI. I am Mimi.

GER. Mimi! Mimi, the smith? And may I ask... are you real, or is this a dream?

MIMI. Is not life a dream?

GER. Yes... but...

MIMI. It is a story. You have to pretend that it is true.

GER. I see!

MIMI. You pretend that it is true... and then you see what happens! It is very interesting!

GER. Yes... I have no doubt. [Peers at him.] And just to help me straighten things out... would you mind telling me... are you old or young?

MIMI. I am young.

GER. How young?

MIMI. Nine hundred years young.

GER. Oh! And why did you come for me?

MIMI. The king commanded it.

GER. The king? And who may this king be?

MIMI. King Alberich.

GER. Alberich. [Stares at the king.] And is this he?

MIMI. It is he.

GER. And may I speak to him?

MIMI. You may.

ALB. Let the earth-man advance. Hail!

GER. Good evening, Alberich.

MIMI. [At his elbow.] Your majesty!

GER. Good evening, your majesty.

ALB. [After along gaze.] You play our music. Where did you learn it?

GER. Why... it's in Wagner's operas. He composed it.

ALB. Humph... composed it!

GER. [Aghast.] You mean he came and copied it!

ALB. Of course!

GER. Why... why... we all thought it was original!

ALB. Original! It is indeed wonderful originality! To listen in the Rhine-depths to the song of the maidens, to dwell in the forest and steal its murmurs, to catch the crackling of the fire and the flowing of the water, the galloping of the wind and the death march of the thunder... and then write it all down for your own! To take our story and tell it just as it happened... to take the very words from our lips, and sign your name to them! Originality!

GER. But, your majesty, one thing at least. Even his enemies granted him that! He invented the invisible orchestra!

ALB. [Laughing.] Have you seen any orchestra here?

[Siegfried motive sounds.]

GER. I hadn't realized it! Do you mean that everything here happens to music?

ALB. If you only had the ears to hear, you would know that the whole world happens to music.

GER. [Stands entranced.] Listen! Listen!

ALB. It is very monotonous, when one is digging out the gold. It keeps up such a wheezing, and pounding.

[Stopped trumpets from orchestra.]

GER. Ah, don't speak of such things! [Gazes about; sees cup.] What is this?

ALB. That is the coronation cup.

GER. The coronation cup?

ALB. One of the greatest of our treasures. It is worth over four hundred thousand dollars. It is the work of the elder Mimi, a most wonderful smith.

GER. [Advancing.] May I look at it?

ALB. You will observe the design of the Rhine maidens.

GER. I can't see it here. It's too dark. Let me have a candle.

MIMI. A candle?

ALL. A candle!

ALB. My dear sir! Candles are so expensive! And why do you want to see it? We never look at our art treasures.

GER. Never look at them!

ALB. No. We know what they are worth, and everyone else knows; and what difference does it make how they look?

GER. Oh, I see!

ALB. Perhaps you would like to see our vaults of gold? [Great excitement among the Nibelungs. The music makes a furious uproar. ALBERICH gives a great key to MIMI, who opens the iron doors.] Approach, sir.

MIMI. Hear the echoes. [Shouts.]

GER. It must be a vast place!

ALB. This particular cavern runs for seventeen miles under the earth.

GER. What! And you mean it is all full of gold?

ALB. From floor to roof with solid masses of it.

GER. Incredible! Is it all of the Nibelung treasure?

ALB. All? Mercy, no! This is simply my own, and I am by no means a rich man. The extent of some of our modern fortunes would simply exceed your belief. We live in an age of enormous productivity. [After a pause.] Will you see more of the vault?

GER. No, I thank you. [They close it.] It must be getting late; and, by the way, your majesty, you know that no one has told me yet why you had me brought here.

ALB. Ah, yes, sure enough. We have business to talk about. Let us get to it! [To MIMI.] Let the hall be cleared. [MIMI drives out the Nibelungs and retires.] Sit on this rock here beside me. [Confidentially.] Now we can talk things over. I trust you are willing to listen to me.

GER. Most certainly. I am very much interested.

ALB. Thank you. You know, my dear sir, that I had a son, Hagen, who was the slayer of the great hero, Siegfried?

GER. Yes, your majesty.

ALB. A most lamentable affair. You did not know, I presume, that Hagen, too, had a son, by one of the daughters of earth?

GER. No. He is not mentioned in history.

ALB. That son, Prince Hagen, is now living; and, in the course of events, he will fall heir to the throne I occupy.

GER. I see.

ALB. The boy is seven or eight hundred years old, which, in your measure, would make him about eighteen. Now, I speak frankly. The boy is wild and unruly. He needs guidance and occupation. And I have sent for you because I understand that you earth-people think more and see farther than we do.

GER. Yes?

ALB. I wish to ask you to help me... to use your strength of mind and body to direct this boy.

GER. But what can I do?

ALB. I wish you to stay here and be Prince Hagen's tutor.

GER. What?

ALB. [Anxiously.] If you will do it, sir, you will carry hence a treasure such as the world has never seen before. And it is a noble work... a great work, sir. He is the grandson of a king! Tell me. .. will you help me?

[Gazes imploringly.]

GER. Let me think. [A pause.] Your majesty, I have things of importance to do, and I have no time to stay here...

ALB. But think of the treasures!

GER. My father is a rich man, and I have no need of treasures. And besides, I am a poet. I have work of my own...

ALB. Oh! don't refuse me, sir!

GER. Listen! There is, perhaps, something else we can do. How would it do to take Prince Hagen up to the world?

ALB. [Starting.] Oh!

GER. This world is a small one. There he might have a wide field for his energies. He might be sent to a good school, and taught the ideals of our Christian civilization.

ALB. [Pondering anxiously.] You mean that you yourself would see to it that proper care was given to him?

GER. If I took him with me it would mean that I was interested in his future.

ALB. It is a startling proposition. What opportunity can you offer him?

GER. I am only a student myself. But my father is a man of importance in the world.

ALB. What does he do?

GER. He is John Isman. They call him the railroad king.

ALB. You have kings in your world, also!

GER. [Smiling.] After a fashion... yes.

ALB. I had not thought of this. I hardly know what to reply. [He starts.] What is that?

[An uproar is heard of left. Shouts and cries; music rises to deafening climax. Nibelungs flee on in terror.]

HAGEN. [Rushes on, struggling wildly, and dragging several Nibelungs.] Let me go, I say! Take off these chains!

ALB. [Rising in seat.] Hagen!

HAGEN. I will not stand it, I tell you!

ALB. Hagen! Listen to me!

HAGEN. No!

ALB. I have something new to tell you. The earth-man has suggested taking you up with him to the world.

HAGEN. [A sudden wild expression flashes across his features.] No! [He gazes from one to the other, half beside himself.] You can't mean it!

ALB. It is true, Hagen.

HAGEN. What... why...

ALB. You would be sent to school and taught the ways of the earth-men. Do you think that you would like to go?

HAGEN. [Wildly.] By the gods! I would!

ALB. [Nervously.] You will promise to obey...

HAGEN. I'll promise anything! I'll do anything!

ALB. Hagen, this is a very grave decision for me. It is such an unusual step! You would have to submit yourself to this gentleman, who is kind enough to take charge of you...

HAGEN. I Will! I will! Quick! [Holding out his chains.] Take them off!

ALB. [Doubtfully.] We can trust you?

HAGEN. You can trust me! You'll have no trouble. Take them off!

ALB. Off with them!

MIMI. [Advances and proceeds to work at chains with a file.] Yes, your majesty.

HAGEN. [TO GERALD.] Tell me! What am I to do?

GER. You are to have an education...

HAGEN. Yes? What's it like? Tell me more about the earth-people.

GER. It's too much to try to tell. You will be there soon.

HAGEN. Ah! Be quick there! [Tears one hand free and waves it.] By the gods!

ALB. [To GERALD.] You had best spend the night with us and consult with me...

HAGEN. No, no! No delay! What's there to consult about?

ALB. We have so much to settle... your clothes... your money...

HAGEN. Give me some gold... that will be all. Let us be off!

GER. I will attend to everything. There is no need of delay.

HAGEN. Come on! [Tears other hand free.] Aha! [Roams about the stage, clenching his hands and gesticulating, while the music rises to a tremendous climax.] Free! Free forever! Aha! Aha! [Turning to GERALD.] Let us be off.

GER. All right. [To ALBERICH.] Good-bye, your majesty.

ALB. [Anxiously.] Good-bye.

HAGEN. Come on!

ALB. [As Nibelungs gather about, waving farewell.] Take care of yourself! Come back to me!

HAGEN. Free! Free! Ha, ha, ha!

MIMI. [With Nibelungs.] Good-bye!

ALB. Good-bye!

GER. Good-bye!

HAGEN. Free!

[Exit, with GERALD, amid chorus of farewells, and wild uproar of music.]

[CURTAIN]

ACT II

[Scene shows the library in a Fifth Avenue mansion; spacious and magnificent. There are folding doors right centre. There is a centre table with a reading lamp and books, and soft leather chairs. The walls are covered with bookcases. An entrance right to drawing-room. Also an entrance left.]

[At rise: GERALD, in evening clothes, reading in front of fire.]

GER. [Stretching, and sighing.] Ah, me! I wish I'd stayed at the club. Bother their dinner parties!

MRS. IS. [Enters right, a nervous, fussy little woman, in evening costume.] Well, Gerald...

GER. Yes, mother?

MRS. IS. You're not coming to dinner?

GER. You don't need me, mother. You've men enough, you said.

MRS. IS. I like to see something of my son now and then.

GER. I had my lunch very late, and I'm honestly not hungry. I'd rather sit and read.

MRS. IS. I declare, Gerald, you run this reading business into the ground. You cut yourself off from everyone.

GER. They don't miss me, mother.

MRS. IS. To-night Renaud is going to give us some crabflake a la Dewey! I told Mrs. Bagley-Willis I'd show her what crabflake could be. She is simply green with envy of our chef.

GER. I fancy that's the reason you invite her, isn't it?

MRS. IS. [Laughs.] Perhaps.

[Exit right. He settles himself to read.]

HICKS. [Enters centre.] Mr. Gerald.

GER. Well?

HICKS. There was a man here to see you some time ago, Sir.

GER. A man to see me? Why didn't you let me know?

HICKS. I started to, Sir. But he disappeared, and I can't find him, Sir.

GER. Disappeared? What do you mean?

HICKS. He came to the side entrance, Sir; and one of the maids answered the bell. He was such a queer-looking chap that she was frightened, and called me. And then I went to ask if you were in, and he disappeared. I wasn't sure if he went out, Sir, or if he was still in the house.

GER. What did he look like?

HICKS. He was a little chap... so high... with a long beard and a humped back...

GER. [Startled.] Mimi!

HICKS. He said you knew him, sir.

GER. Yes! I would have seen him.

HICKS. I didn't know, sir...

GER. Watch out for him. He'll surely come back.

HICKS. Yes, Sir. I'm very sorry, sir.

[Exit centre.]

GER. [To himself.] Mimi! What can that mean?

Mimi. [Opens door, left, and peeps in.] Ha!

GER. [Starts.] Mimi!

MIMI. Ssh!

GER. What is it?

MIMI. Where is Prince Hagen?

GER. I don't know.

MIMI. You don't know?

GER. No.

MIMI. But I must see him!

GER. I've no idea where he is.

MIMI. But... you promised to take care of him!

GER. Yes... and I tried to. But he ran away...

MIMI. What?

GER. I've not heard of him for two years now.

MIMI. [Coming closer.] Tell me about it.

GER. I took him to a boarding school... a place where he'd be taken care of and taught. And he rebelled... he would not obey anyone.. . [Takes some faded telegrams from pocket book.] See! This is what I got.

MIMI. What are they?

GER. Telegrams they sent me. [Reads.] Hagen under physical restraint. Whole school disorganized. Come immediately and take him away.

MIMI. Ha!

GER. That's one. And here's the other: Hagen has escaped, threatening teachers with revolver. Took train for New York. What shall we do? [Puts away papers.] And that's all.

MIMI. All?

GER. That was over two years ago. And I've not heard of him since.

MIMI. But he must be found!

GER. I have tried. I can't.

MIMI. [Vehemently.] But we cannot do without him!

GER. What's the matter?

MIMI. I cannot tell you. But we must have him! The people need him!

GER. He has lost himself in this great city. What can I do?

MIMI. He must be found. [Voices heard centre.] What is that?

GER. It is some company.

MIMI. [Darts left.] We must find Prince Hagen! He must come back to Nibelheim!

[Exit left.]

MRS. BAGLEY-WILLIS. [Off centre.] It was crabflake a la Dewey she promised me!

[Enters with ISMAN.]

GER. How do you do, Mrs. Bagley-Willis?

MRS. B.-W. How do you do, Gerald?

GER. Hello, father!

ISMAN. Hello, Gerald!

MRS. B.-W. Am I the first to arrive?

GER. I think so.

MRS. B.-W. And how is Estelle after her slumming adventure?

GER. She's all right.

ISMAN. That was a fine place for you to take my daughter!

MRS. B.-W. It wasn't my fault. She would go. And her mother consented.

GER. I wish I'd been there with you.

MRS. B.-W. Indeed, I wished for someone. I was never more frightened in my life.

ISMAN. Did you see this morning's Record?

MRS. B.-W. No. What?

ISMAN. About that fellow, Steve O'Hagen?

MRS. B.-W. Good heavens!

GER. Nothing about Estelle, I hope!

ISMAN. No... apparently nobody noticed that incident. But about his political speech, and the uproar he's making on the Bowery. They say the streets were blocked for an hour... the police couldn't clear them.

GER. He must be an extraordinary talker.

MRS. B.-W. You can't imagine it. The man is a perfect demon!

GER. Where does he come from?

ISMAN. Apparently nobody knows. The papers say he turned up a couple of years ago... he won't talk about his past. He joined Tammany Hall, and he's sweeping everything before him.

GER. What do you suppose will come of it?

ISMAN. Oh, he'll get elected... what is it he's to be... an alderman?... and then he'll sell out, like all the rest. I was talking about it this afternoon, with Plimpton and Rutherford.

MRS. B.-W. They're to be here to-night, I understand.

ISMAN. Yes... so they mentioned. Ah! Here's Estelle!

ESTELLE. [Enters, centre, with an armful of roses.] Ah! Mrs. Bagley-Willis! Good evening!

MRS. B.-W. Good evening, Estelle.

EST. Good evening, father. Hello, Gerald.

GER. My, aren't we gorgeous to-night!

EST. Just aren't we!

MRS. B.-W. The adventure doesn't seem to have hurt you. Where is your mother?

GER. She went into the drawing-room. [MRS. B.-W. and ISMAN go off, right; ESTELLE is about to follow.] Estelle!

EST. What is it?

GER. What's this I hear about your adventure last night?

EST. [With sudden seriousness.] Oh, Gerald! [Comes closer.] It was a frightful thing! I've hardly dared to think about it!

GER. Tell me.

EST. Gerald, that man was talking straight at me... he meant every bit of it for me!

GER. Tell me the story.

EST. Why, you know, Lord Alderdyce had heard about this wild fellow, Steve O'Hagen, who's made such a sensation this campaign. And he's interested in our election and wanted to hear O'Hagen speak. He said he had a friend who'd arrange for us to be introduced to him; and so we went down there. And there was a most frightful crowd... it was an outdoor meeting, you know. We pushed our way into a saloon, where the mob was shouting around this O'Hagen. And then he caught sight of us... and Gerald, from the moment he saw me he never took his eyes off me! Never once!

GER. [Smiling.] Well, Estelle... you've been looked at before.

EST. Ah, but never like that!

GER. What sort of a man is he?

EST. He's small and dark and ugly... he wore a rough reefer and cap ... but Gerald, he's no common man! There's something strange and terrible about him... there's a fire blazing in him. The detective who was with us introduced us to him... and he stood there and stared at me! I tried to say something or other... "I've been so interested in your speech, Mr. O'Hagen." And he laughed at me... "Yes, I've no doubt." And then suddenly... it was as if he leaped at me! He pointed his finger straight into my face, and his eyes fairly shone. "Wait for me! I'll be with you! I'm coming to the top!"

GER. Good God!

EST. Imagine it! I was simply paralyzed! "Mark what I tell you," he went on... "it'll be of interest to you some day to remember it. You may wait for me! I'm coming! You will not escape me!"

GER. Why... he's mad!

EST. He was like a wild beast. Everybody in the place was staring at us as he rushed on. "You have joy and power and freedom... all the privileges of life... all things that are excellent and beautiful. You are born to them... you claim them! And you come down here to stare at us as you might at some strange animals in a cage. You chatter and laugh and go your way... but remember what I told you. .. I shall be with you! You cannot keep ME down! I shall be master of you all!"

GER. Incredible!

EST. And then in a moment it was all over. He made a mocking bow to the party... "It has given me the greatest pleasure in the world to meet you!" And with a wild laugh he went out of the door... and the crowd in the street burst into a roar that was like a clap of thunder. [A pause.] Gerald, what do you think he meant?

GER. My dear, you've been up against the class-war. It's rather the fashion now, you know.

EST. Oh, but it was horrible! I can't get it out of my mind. We heard some of his speech afterwards... and it seemed as if every word of it was meant for me! He lashed the crowd to a perfect fury... I think they'd have set fire to the city if he'd told them to. What do you suppose he expects to do?

GER. I can't imagine, I'm sure.

EST. I should like to know more about him. He was never raised in the slums, I feel certain.

GER. Steve O'Hagen. The name sounds Irish.

EST. I don't think he's Irish. He's dark and strange-looking... almost uncanny.

GER. I shall go down there and hear him the first chance I get. And now, I guess I'd best get out, if I want to dodge old Plimpton.

EST. Yes... and Rutherford, too. Isn't it a bore! I think they are perfectly odious people.

GER. Why do you suppose mother invited them?

EST. Oh, it's a business affair... they have forced their way into some deal of father's, and so we have to cultivate them.

GER. Plimpton, the coal baron! And Rutherford, the steel king! I wonder how many hundred millions of dollars we shall have to have before we can choose our guests for something more interesting than their Wall Street connections!

EST. I think I hear them. [Listens.] Yes... the voice. [Mocking PLIMPTON'S manner and tone.] Good evening, Miss Isman. I guess I'll skip it!

[Exit right.]

GER. And I, too!

[Exit left.]

RUTHERFORD. [A stout and rather coarse-looking man, enters, right, with PLIMPTON.] It's certainly an outrageous state of affairs, Plimpton!

PLIMPTON. [A thin, clerical-looking person, with square-cut beard.] Disgraceful! Disgraceful!

RUTH. The public seems to be quite hysterical!

PLIMP. We have got to a state where simply to be entrusted with great financial responsibility is enough to constitute a man a criminal; to warrant a newspaper in prying into the intimate details of his life, and in presenting him in hideous caricatures.

RUTH. I can sympathize with you, Plimpton... these government investigations are certainly a trial. [Laughing.] I've had my turn at them... I used to lie awake nights trying to remember what my lawyers had told me to forget!

PLIMP. Ahem! Ahem! Yes... a rather cynical jest! I can't say exactly...

MRS. IS. [In doorway, right.] Ah, Mr. Plimpton! How do you do? And Mr. Rutherford?

PLIMP. Good evening, Mrs. Isman.

RUTH. Good evening, Mrs. Isman.

MRS. IS. You managed to tear yourself away from business cares, after all!

PLIMP. It was not easy, I assure you.

MRS. IS. Won't you come in?

RUTH. With pleasure.

[Exit, right, with MRS. ISMAN, followed by PLIMPTON.]

GER. [Enters, left.] That pious old fraud! [Sits in chair.] Well, I'm safe for a while!

[Sprawls at ease and reads.]

HICKS. [Enters, centre.] A gentleman to see you, Mr. Gerald.

GER. Hey? [Takes card, looks, then gives violent start.] Prince Hagen! [Stands aghast, staring; whispers, half dazed.] Prince Hagen!

HICKS. [After waiting.] What shall I tell him, sir?

GER. What... what does he look like?

HICKS. Why... he seems to be a gentleman, sir.

GER. How is he dressed?

HICKS. For dinner, sir.

GER. [Hesitates, gazes about nervously.] Bring him here... quickly!

HICKS. Yes, sir.

GER. And shut the door afterwards.

HICKS. Yes, sir.

[Exit.]

GER. [Stands staring.] Prince Hagen! He's come at last!

[Takes the faded telegrams from his pocket; looks at them; then goes to door, right, and closes it.]

HICKS. [Enters, centre.] Prince Hagen.

HAGEN. [Enters; serene and smiling, immaculately clad.] Ah, Gerald!

GER. [Gazing.] Prince Hagen!

HAGEN. You are surprised to see me!

GER. I confess that I am.

HAGEN. Did you think I was never coming back?

GER. I had given you up.

HAGEN. Well, here I am... to report progress.

GER. [After a pause.] Where have you been these two years?

HAGEN. Oh, I've been seeing life...

GER. You didn't like the boarding school?

HAGEN. [With sudden vehemence.] Did you think I would like it? Did you think I'd come to this world to have my head stuffed with Latin conjugations and sawdust?

GER. I had hoped that in a good Christian home...

HAGEN. [Laughing.] No, no, Gerald! I let you talk that sort of thing to me in the beginning. It sounded fishy even then, but I didn't say anything... I wanted to get my bearings. But I hadn't been twenty-four hours in that good Christian home before I found out what a kettleful of jealousies and hatreds it was. The head master was an old sap-head; and the boys!... I was strange and ugly, and they thought they could torment and bully me; but I fought 'em... by the Lord, I fought 'em day and night, I fought 'em all around the place! And when I'd mastered 'em, you should have seen how they cringed and toadied! They hated the slavery they lived under, but not one of them dared raise his hand against it.

GER. Well, you've seen the world in your own way. Now are you ready to go back to Nibelheim?

HAGEN. Good God, no!

GER. You know it's my duty to send you back.

HAGEN. Oh, say! My dear fellow!

GER. You know the solemn promise I made to King Alberich.

HAGEN. Yes... but you can't carry it out.

GER. But I can!

HAGEN. How?

GER. I could invoke the law, if need be. You know you are a minor...

HAGEN. My dear boy, I'm over seven hundred years old!

GER. Ah, but that is a quibble. You know that in our world that is only equal to about eighteen...

HAGEN. I have read up the law, but I haven't found any provision for reducing Nibelung ages to your scale.

GER. But you can't deny...

HAGEN. I wouldn't need to deny. The story's absurd on the face of it. You know perfectly well that there are no such things as Nibelungs! [GERALD gasps.] And besides, you're a poet, and everybody knows you're crazy. Fancy what the newspaper reporters would do with such a yarn! [Cheerfully.] Come, old man, forget about it, and let's be friends. You'll have a lot more fun watching my career. And besides, what do you want? I've come back, and I'm ready to follow your advice.

GER. How do you mean?

HAGEN. You told me to stay in school until I'd got my bearings in the world. And then I was to have a career. Well, I've got my education for myself... and now I'm ready for the career. [After a pause.] Listen, Gerald. I said I'd be a self-made man. I said I'd conquer the world for myself. But of late I've come to realize how far it is to the top, and I can't spare the time.

GER. I see.

HAGEN. And then... besides that... I've met a woman.

GER. [Startled.] Good heavens!

HAGEN. Yes. I'm in love.

GER. But surely... you don't expect to marry!

HAGEN. Why not? My mother was an earth-woman, and her mother, also.

GER. To be sure. I'd not realized it. [A pause.] Who is the woman?

HAGEN. I don't know. I only know she belongs in this world of yours. And I've come to seek her out. I shall get her, never fear!

GER. What are your plans?

HAGEN. I've looked this Christian civilization of yours over... and I'm prepared to play the game. You can take me up and put me into Society... as you offered to do before. You'll find that I'll do you credit.

GER. But such a career requires money.

HAGEN. Of course. Alberich will furnish it, if you tell him it's needed. You must call Mimi.

GER. Mimi is here now.

HAGEN. [Starting.] What!

GER. He is in the house.

HAGEN. For what?

GER. He came to look for you.

HAGEN. What is the matter?

GER. I don't know. He wants you to return to Nibelheim.

HAGEN. Find him. Let me see him!

GER. All right. Wait here.

[Exit left.]

HAGEN. What can that mean?

EST. [Enters, right, sees PRINCE HAGEN, starts wildly and screams.] Ah! [She stands transfixed; a long pause.] Steve O'Hagen! [A pause.] Steve O'Hagen! What does it mean?

HAGEN. Who are you?

EST. I live here.

HAGEN. Your name?

EST. Estelle Isman.

HAGEN. [In a transport of amazement.] Estelle Isman! You are Gerald's sister!

EST. Yes.

HAGEN. By the gods!

EST. [Terrified.] You know my brother!

HAGEN. Yes.

EST. You... Steve O'Hagen!

HAGEN. [Gravely.] I am Prince Hagen

EST. Prince Hagen!

HAGEN. A foreign nobleman.

EST. What... what do you mean? You were on the Bowery!

HAGEN. I came to this country to study its institutions. I wished to know them for myself... therefore I went into politics. Don't you see?

EST! [Dazed.] I see!

HAGEN. Now I am on the point of giving up the game and telling the story of my experiences.

EST. What are you doing here... in this house?

HAGEN. I came for you.

EST. [Stares at him.] How dare you?

HAGEN. I would dare anything for you! [They gaze at each other.] Don't you understand?

EST. [Vehemently.] No! No! I am afraid of you! You have no business to be here!

HAGEN. [Taking a step towards her.] Listen...

EST. No! I will not hear you! You cannot come here!

[Stares at him, then abruptly exit, centre.]

HAGEN. [Laughs.] Humph! [Hearing voices.] Who is this?

RUTH. [Off right.] I don't agree with you.

IS. Nor I, either, Plimpton. [Enters with PLIMPTON and RUTHERFORD; sees HAGEN.] Oh... I beg your pardon.

HAGEN. I am waiting for your son, Sir.

IS. I see. Won't you be seated?

HAGEN. I thank you. [Sits at ease in chair.]

PLIM. My point is, it's as Lord Alderdyce says... we have no hereditary aristocracy in this country, no traditions of authority... nothing to hold the mob in check.

IS. There is the constitution.

PLIM. They may over-ride it.

IS. There are the courts.

PLIM. They may defy the courts.

RUTH. Oh, Plimpton, that's absurd!

PLIM. Nothing of the kind, Rutherford! Suppose they were to elect to office some wild and reckless demagog... take, for instance, that ruffian you were telling us about... down there on the Bowery... [HAGEN starts, and listens] and he were to defy the law and the courts? He is preaching just that to the mob... striving to rouse the elemental wild beast in them! And some day they will pour out into this avenue...

RUTH. [Vehemently.] Very well, Plimpton! Let them come! Have we not the militia and the regulars? We could sweep the avenue with one machine gun...

PLIM. But suppose the troops would not fire?

RUTH. But that is impossible!

PLIM. Nothing of the kind, Rutherford! No, no... we must go back of all that! It is in the hearts of the people that we must erect our defenses. It is the spirit of this godless and skeptical age that is undermining order. We must teach the people the truths of religion. We must inculcate lessons of sobriety and thrift, of reverence for constituted authority. We must set our faces against these new preachers of license and infidelity... we must go back to the old-time faith... to love, and charity, and self-sacrifice...

HAGEN. [Interrupting.] That's it! You've got it there!

IS. [Amazed.] Why...

PLIM. Sir?

HAGEN. You've said it! Set the parsons after them! Teach them heaven! Set them to singing about harps and golden crowns, and milk and honey flowing! Then you can shut them up in slums and starve them, and they won't know the difference. Teach them non-resistance and self-renunciation! You've got the phrases all pat... handed out from heaven direct! Take no thought saying what ye shall eat! Lay not up for yourselves treasures on earth! Render unto Caesar the things that are Caesar's!

IS. Why... this is preposterous!

PLIM. This is blasphemy!

HAGEN. You're Plimpton... Plimpton, the coal baron, I take it. I know you by your pictures. You shut up little children by tens of thousands to toil for you in the bowels of the earth. You crush your rivals, and form a trust, and screw up prices to freeze the poor in winter! And you... [to RUTHERFORD] you're Rutherford, the steel king, I take it. You have slaves working twelve hours a day and seven days a week in your mills. And you mangle them in hideous accidents, and then cheat their widows of their rights... and then you build churches, and set your parsons to preach to them about love and self-sacrifice! To teach them charity, while you crucify justice! To trick them with visions of an imaginary paradise, while you pick their pockets upon earth! To put arms in their hands, and send them to shoot their brothers, in the name of the Prince of Peace!

RUTH. This is outrageous!

PLIM. [Clenching his fists.] Infamous scoundrel!

RUTH. [Advancing Upon HAGEN.] How dare you!

HAGEN. It stings, does it? Ha! Ha!

PLIM. [Sputtering.] You wretch!

IS. This has gone too far. Stop, Rutherford! Calm yourself, Plimpton. Let us not forget ourselves! [To PRINCE HAGEN, haughtily.] I do not know who you are, sir, or by what right you are in my house. You say that you are a friend of my son's...

HAGEN. I claim that honor, sir.

IS. The fact that you claim it prevents my ordering you into the street. But I will see my son, sir, and find out by what right you are here to insult my guests. [Turning.] Come, Plimpton. Come, Rutherford ... we will bandy no words with him!

[They go off, centre.]

HAGEN. [Alone.] By God! I touched them! Ha, ha, ha! [Grimly.] He will
order me into the street! [With concentrated fury.] That is it!
They shut you out! They build a wall about themselves! Aristocracy!
[Clenching his fast.] Very well! So be it! You sit within your fortress
of privilege! You are haughty and contemptuous, flaunting your power!
But I'll breach your battlements, I'll lay them in the dust! I'll bring
you to your knees before me!

[A silence. Suddenly there is heard, very faintly, the Nibelung theme.
It is repeated; HAGEN starts.]

MIMI. [Enters, left.] Prince Hagen!

HAGEN. Mimi!

MIMI. At last!

HAGEN. [Approaching.] What is it?

MIMI. [Beckons.] Come here.

HAGEN. [In excitement.] What do you want?

MIMI. You must come back!

HAGEN. What do you mean?

MIMI. The people want you.

HAGEN. What for?

MIMI. They need you. You must be king.

HAGEN. [Wildly.] Ha?

MIMI. Alberich...

HAGEN. Alberich?

MIMI. He is dead!

HAGEN. [With wild start.] Dead!

MIMI. Yes... he died last night!

HAGEN. [Turns pale and staggers; then leaps at Mimi, clutching him by the arm.] No! NO!

MIMI. It is true.

HAGEN. My God! [A look of wild, drunken rapture crosses his face; he clenches his hands and raises his arms.] Ha, ha, ha!

MIMI. [Shrinks in horror.] Prince Hagen!

HAGEN. He is dead! He is dead! [Leaps at mimi.] The gold?

MIMI. The gold is yours.

HAGEN. Ha, ha, ha! It is mine! It is mine! [Begins pacing the floor wildly.] Victory! Victory! VICTORY! Ha, ha, ha! Ha, ha, ha! [Spreads out his arms, with a triumphant shout.] I have them! By God! Isman! Plimpton and Rutherford! Estelle! I have them all! It is triumph! It is glory! It is the world! I am King! I am King! King! KING! [Seizes MIMI and starts centre; the music rises to climax.] To Nibelheim! To Nibelheim! [Stands stretching out his arms in exultation; a wild burst of music.] Make way for Hagen! Make way for Hagen!

[CURTAIN]

ACT III

[The conservatory is a study in green and gold, with strange tropical plants having golden flowers. There are entrances right and left. In the centre, up-stage, is a niche with a gold table and a couple of gold chairs, and behind these a stand with the "coronation cup"; to the right the golden throne from Nibelheim, and to the left a gold fountain splashing gently.] [At rise: The stage is empty. The strains of an orchestra heard from ball-room, left.]

MRS. BAGLEY-WILLIS. [Enters, right, with DE WIGGLESTON RIGGS; she wears
a very low-cut gown, a stomacher and tiara of diamonds, and numerous ropes of pearls.] Well, Wiggie, he has made a success of it!

DE WIGGLESTON RIGGS. [Petit and exquisite.] He was certain to make a success when Mrs. Bagley-Willis took him up!

MRS. B.-W. But he wouldn't do a single thing I told him. I never had such a protege in my life!

DE W. R. Extraordinary!

MRS. B.-W. I told him it would be frightfully crude, and it is. And yet, Wiggie, it's impressive, in its way... nobody can miss the feeling. Such barbaric splendor!

DE W. R. The very words! Barbaric splendor!

MRS. B.-W. I never heard of anything like it... the man simply poured out money. It's quite in a different class from other affairs.

DE W. R. [Holding up his hands.] Stupefying!

MRS. B.-W. And did you ever know the public to take such interest in a social event? People haven't even stopped to think about the panic in Wall Street.

DE W. R. I assure you, Mrs. Bagley-Willis, it begins a new epoch in our social history. [To LORD ALDERDYCE, who enters, left, with GERALD.] How do you do, Lord Alderdyce?

MRS. B.-W. Good evening, Lord Alderdyce. Good evening, Gerald.

LORD A. Good evening, Mrs. Bagley-Willis. Good evening, Mr. Riggs.

GERALD. Good evening, Wiggie! [DE W. R. and MRS. B.-W. move toward left.] I suppose that old lady's taken to herself all the credit for this evening's success!

LORD A. Well, really, you know, wasn't it... ah... quite a feat to make society swallow this adventurer?

GERALD. How can anybody stay away? When a man spends several millions on a single entertainment people have to come out of pure curiosity.

LORD A. To be sure! I did, anyway!

GER. [Gazing about.] Think of buying all the old Vandergrift palaces at one swoop!

LORD A. Oh, really!

GER. This palace was one of the landmarks of the city; all its decorations had been taken from old palaces in Italy. And he tore everything off and gave it away to a museum, and he made it over in three months!

LORD A. Amazing. [Music and applause heard left.]

MRS. B.-W. Mazzanini must be going to sing again.

DE W. R. Let us go!

MRS. B.-W. Fancy opera stars to dance to! A waltz song at a thousand dollars a minute!

DE W. R. Ah, but SUCH a song!

[They go off, left; half a dozen guests enter, right, and cross in groups.]

RUTH. [Enters, right, with PLIMPTON; looking about.] An extraordinary get-up!

PLIMP. Appalling extravagance, Rutherford! Appalling!

RUTH. Practically everybody's here.

PLIMP. Everybody I ever heard of.

RUTH. One doesn't meet you at balls very often, Plimpton.

PLIM. No. To tell the truth, I came from motives of prudence.

RUTH. Humph! To tell the truth, so did I!

PLIM. The man is mad, you know... and one can't tell what might offend him!

RUTH. And with the market in such a state!

PLIM. It's terrible! Terrible!... ah, Lord Alderdyce!

LORD A. Good evening, Mr. Plimpton. How d'ye do, Mr. Rutherford?

RUTH. As well as could be expected, Lord Alderdyce. It's a trying time for men of affairs. [They pass on, and go of, left.]

GER. They must be under quite a strain just now.

LORD A. Don't mention it. Don't mention it! I've invested all my funds in this country, and I tremble to pick up the last edition of the paper!

MRS. IS. [Enters, right, costumed en grande dame, much excited.] Oh, Gerald, Lord Alderdyce, what do you think I've just heard?

LORD A. What?

MRS. IS. About Prince Hagen and Mrs. Bagley-Willis... how she came to take him up! Percy Pennington told me about it... he's her own first cousin, you know, Lord Alderdyce... and he vows he saw the letter in her desk!

LORD A. Oh, tell us!

MRS. IS. Well, it was just after Prince Hagen made his appearance, when the papers were printing pages about him. And the news came that he'd bought these palaces; and the next day Mrs. Bagley-Willis got a letter marked personal. Percy quoted the words... Dear Madam: I wish to enter Society. I have no time to go through with the usual formalities. I am a nobleman, with an extraordinary mind and unlimited money. I intend to entertain New York Society as it has never dreamed of being entertained before. I should be very pleased if you would co-operate with me in making my opening ball a success. If you are prepared to do this, I am prepared to pay you the sum of one million dollars cash as soon as I receive your acceptance. Needless to say, of course, this proposition is entirely confidential!

LORD. A. By jove!

MRS. IS. Think of it!

GER. But can it be true?

MRS. IS. What is more likely, my dear? You know that Mrs. Bagley-Willis has been spending millions every season to entertain at Newport; and their fortune will never stand that! Oh, I must give it to Van Tribber... he'll see that the papers have it!

LORD A. But hadn't you better make sure that it's really...

MRS. IS. It doesn't make the slightest difference! Everybody will know that it's true!

GER. They are ready to believe anything about Prince Hagen.

MRS. IS. Certainly, after a glimpse of this palace. Did you ever see such frantic money-spending in your life?

LORD A. Never!

MRS. IS. Gold! Gold! I am positively blinded with the sight of gold. I'd seen every kind of decoration and furniture, I thought... but solid gold is new to me!

LORD A. Just look at this cup, for instance! [Points to coronation cup.] And those fountains... I believe that even the basins are of gold.

MRS. IS. Perhaps we could stop the water and see.

LORD A. I must go... I have a dance. I am sorry not to see your daughter.

MRS. IS. Yes... it was too bad she couldn't come. Good-bye. [LORD ALDERDYCE exit.]

MRS. IS. [Pointing to throne.] Look at that thing, Gerald!

GER. Yes... no wonder the crowd came!

MRS. IS. I imagine a good many came because they didn't dare stay away. They certainly can't be enjoying themselves after such a day down town.

GER. It was too bad the panic should come just on the eve of the ball.

MRS. IS. My dear Gerald! That's his sense of humor! He wanted to bring them here and set them to dancing and grinning, while in their hearts they are frightened to death.

GER. How did he do it, anyway?

MRS. IS. Why, he seems to have money without limit... and he's been buying and buying... everything in sight! You know how prices have been soaring the past two months. And of course the public went wild, and took to speculating. Then Prince Hagen sold; and the bottom has simply dropped out of everything.

GER. I see. And do you suppose the slump has hit father?

MRS. IS. I don't know. He won't talk to me about it. But it's easy to see how distressed he is. And then, to cap the climax, Estelle refuses to come here! Prince Hagen is certain to be furious.

GER. For my part, I admire her courage.

MRS. IS. But, Gerald... we can't afford to defy this man.

GER. Estelle can afford it, I hope.

MRS. IS. Here comes your father now. Look at him! Gerald, won't you go, please... I want to have a talk with him.

GER. All right. [Exit, right.]

MRS. IS. John!

ISMAN. [Enters, left, pale and depressed.] What is it?

MRS. IS. You look so haggard and worried!

IS. I AM worried!

MRS. IS. You ought to be home in bed.

IS. I couldn't sleep. What good would it do?

MRS. IS. Aren't you going to get any rest at all?

IS. It's time for reports from the London markets pretty soon. They open at five o'clock, by our time. And I'm hoping there may be some support for Intercontinental... it's my last hope.

MRS. IS. Oh, dear me! Dear me!

IS. If that fails, there is nothing left for us. We are ruined! Utterly ruined!

MRS. IS. John!

IS. We shall be paupers!

MRS. IS. John Isman, that's absurd! A man who's worth a hundred million dollars, like you...

IS. It'll be gone... all of it!

MRS. IS. Gone?

Is. Do you realize that to-day I had to sell every dollar of my Transatlantic stock?

MRS. IS. [Horrified.] Good God!

IS. There has never been a day like it in all history! There are no words to tell about it!

MRS. IS. Oh, that monster!

IS. And the worst of it is, the man seems to be after me particularly! Everything I rely upon seems to collapse... everywhere I turn I find that I'm blocked.

MRS. IS. Oh, it must have been because of that affair in our house.. . and in the saloon that dreadful night. We ought never to have gone to that place! I knew as soon as I laid eyes on the man that he'd do us harm.

IS. We must keep out of his power. We must save what we can from the wreck and learn to do with it. You'll have to give up your Newport plans this year.

MRS. IS. [Aghast.] What!

IS. We won't be able to open the house.

MRS. IS. You're mad!

IS. My dear...

MRS. IS. Now, John Isman, you listen to me! I was quite sure you had some such idea in your mind! And I tell you right now, I simply will not hear of it! I...

IS. But what can we do, my dear?

MRS. IS. I don't know what we can do! But you'll have to raise money somehow. I will not surrender my social position to Mrs. Bagley-Willis ... not for all the Wall Street panics in the world. Oh, that man is a fiend! I tell you, John Isman...

IS. Control yourself!

HAGEN. [Off right.] Very well! I shall be charmed, I'm sure. [Enters.] Oh! How do you do, Mrs. Isman?

MRS. IS. Oh, Prince Hagen, a most beautiful evening you've given us.

HAGEN. Ah! I'm glad if you've enjoyed it.

MRS. IS. Yes, indeed...

IS. Prince Hagen, may I have a few words with you?

HAGEN. Why, surely... if you wish...

IS. I do.

MRS. IS. Prince Hagen will excuse me. [Exit, left.]

HAGEN. [Goes to table, centre, and sits opposite ISMAN.] Well?

IS. Prince Hagen, what do you want with me?

HAGEN. [Surprised.] Why... the pleasure of your company.

IS. I mean in the Street.

HAGEN. Oh! Have you been hit?

IS. Don't mock me. You have used your resources deliberately to ruin me. You have followed me... you have taken every railroad in which I am interested, and driven it to the wall. And I ask you, man to man, what do you want?

HAGEN. [After some thought.] Isman, listen to me. You remember four months ago I offered you a business alliance?

IS. I had no idea of your resources then. Had I known, I should not have rejected your offer. Am I being punished for that?

HAGEN. No, Isman... it isn't punishment. Had you gone into the alliance with me it would have been just the same. It was my purpose to get you into my power.

IS. Oh!

HAGEN. To bring you here... to make you sit down before me, and ask, What do you want?... And so I will tell you what I want, man to man! [A pause.] I want your daughter.

IS. [Starts.] What!

HAGEN. I want your daughter.

IS. Good God!

HAGEN. Do you understand now?

IS. [Whispering.] I understand!

HAGEN. Isman, you are a man of the world, and we can talk together. I love your daughter, and I wish to make her my wife.

IS. And so you ruined me!

HAGEN. Four months ago I was an interloper and an adventurer. In a month or two I shall be the master of your financial and political world. Then I had nothing to offer your daughter. Now I can make her the first lady of the land.

IS. But, man, we don't sell our children... not in America.

HAGEN. Don't talk to me like a fool, Isman. I never have anything to do with your shams.

IS. But the girl! She must consent!

HAGEN. I'll attend to that. Meantime, I want you to know what I mean. On the day that your daughter marries me I will put you at the head of my interests, and make you the second richest man in America. You understand?

IS. [Weakly.] I understand.

HAGEN. Very well. And don't forget to tell your wife about it. [He rises.]

IS. Is that all?

HAGEN. No; one thing more. Your daughter is not here to-night.

IS. No.

HAGEN. I wish her to come.

IS. But... she is indisposed!

HAGEN. That is a pretext. She did not want to come.

IS. Possibly...

HAGEN. Tell her to come.

IS. [Startled.] What? Now? It is too late!

HAGEN. Nonsense. Your home is only a block away. Telephone to her.

IS. [Dismayed.] But... she will not be ready.

HAGEN. Tell her to come! Whatever she is wearing, she will outshine them all. [ISMAN hesitates a moment, as if to speak, then goes off, right, half dazed; the other watches him, laughing silently to himself.] That's all right! [Sees Calkins.] Ah, Calkins!

CALKINS. [Enters with an armful of papers.] Here are the morning papers, Prince.

HAGEN. Ah! [Takes them.] Still moist! Did you think I wanted them that badly?

CAL. Promptness never harms.

HAGEN. [Opening papers.] That's true. Ah, they hardly knew which was more important... the ball or the panic! We filled them up pretty full. Did you see if they followed the proofs?

CAL. There are no material changes.

HAGEN. Ha! Ha! Cartoons! Prince Hagen invites the Four Hundred with one hand and knocks them down with the other! Pretty good! Pretty good! What's this? Three millions to decorate his palaces... half a million for a single ball?

CAL. I suppose they couldn't credit the figures.

HAGEN. Humph! We'll educate them! [Sweeps papers out of the way.] So much for that! Were all the orders for the London opening gone over?

CAL. All correct, Prince.

HAGEN. Very good! That's all. [CAL. exit.] They're all anxious about London... I can see it! Ah, Gerald!

GER. [Enters, right.] Hello!

HAGEN. [Smiling.] You see, they came to my party!

GER. Yes.

HAGEN. They smile and chatter... they bow and cringe to me... and I have not preached any of your Christian virtues, either!

GER. No. I grant it. It's a very painful sight. [After a pause.] That was a pleasant fancy... to have a panic on the eve of your ball!

HAGEN. It wasn't nearly as bad as I meant it to be. Wait and see today's!

GER. What's the end of it all?

HAGEN. The end? Why have an end? I didn't make this game... I play it according to other men's rules. I buy and sell stocks, and make what money I can. The end may take care of itself.

GER. It's rather hard on the helpless people, isn't it?

HAGEN. Humph! The people! [After a pause.] Gerald, this world of yours has always seemed to me like a barrel full of rats. There's only room for a certain number on top, and the rest must sweat for it till they die.

GER. It's not a very pleasant image to think of.

HAGEN. I don't think of it. I simply happen to find myself on top, and I stay there and enjoy the view. [Seats himself at table.] As a matter of fact, Gerald, one of the things I intend to do with this world is to clean it up. Don't imagine that I will tolerate such stupid waste as we have at present... everybody trying to cheat everybody else, and nobody to keep the streets clean. It's as if a dozen mere should go out into a field to catch a horse, and spend all their time in trying to keep each other from catching it. When I take charge they'll catch the horse.

GER. [Drily.] And you'll ride him.

HAGEN. And I'll ride him. [Laughs.]

GER. [After a pause.] At first I couldn't make out why you bothered with this Society game. Now I begin to understand. You wanted to see them!

HAGEN. I wanted to watch them wriggle! I wanted to take them, one by one, and strip off their shams! Take that fellow Rutherford, the steel man! Or Plimpton, the coal baron, casting his eyes up to heaven, and singing psalms through his nose! The instant I laid eyes on that whining old hypocrite, I hated him; and I vowed I'd never rest again till I'd shown him as he is... a coward and a knave! And I tell you, Gerald, before I get through with him... Ah, there he is!

PLIM. [Off.] Hello, Isman!

HAGEN. Come. [Draws back with GERALD.]

IS. [Entering, right, with PLIMPTON and RUTHERFORD.] Any word yet?

PLIM. Nothing yet!

RUTH. Such a night as this has been!

IS. If the thing keeps up today the Exchange will have to close... there will be no help for it.

PLIM. We are in the hands of a madman!

RUTH. We must have a conference with him... we must find out what he wants.

IS. Did you speak to him, Plimpton?

PLIM. I tried to. I might as well have butted my head against a stone wall. "I have money," he said, "and I wish to buy and sell stocks. Isn't that my right?"

RUTH. He's a fiend! A fiend!

PLIM. He smiled as he shook my hand... and he knows that if coal stocks go down another ten points I'll be utterly ruined!

IS. Terrible! Terrible!

PLIM. [To RUTHERFORD.] Rutherford, have you learned any more about where his money comes from?

RUTH. I meant to tell you... I've had another report. The mystery deepens every hour. It's always the same thing... the man takes a train and goes out into the country; he gathers all the wagons for miles around, and goes to some place in the woods... and there is a pile of gold, fifty tons of it, maybe, covered over with brush. Nobody knows how it got there, nobody has time to ask. He loads it into the wagons, takes it aboard the train, and brings it to the Sub-treasury.

IS. The man's an alchemist! He's been manufacturing it and getting ready.

RUTH. Perhaps. Who can tell? All I know is the Sub-treasury has bought over two billion dollars' worth of gold bullion in the last four months... and what can we do in the face of that?

PLIM. No wonder that prices went up to the skies!

RUTH. I had the White House on the 'phone this afternoon. We can demonetize gold... the government can refuse to buy any more.

IS. But then what would become of credit?

PLIM. [Vehemently.] No, no... that will not help! [Gazes about nervously.] There's only one thing. [Whispers.] That man must be killed!

RUTH. [Horrified.] Ah!

IS. No.

PLIM. Just that! Nothing else will help! And instantly... or it will be too late.

IS. Plimpton!

PLIM. He must not be alive when the Exchange opens this morning!

RUTH. But how?

PLIM. I don't know... but we must find a way! We owe it as a public duty... the man is a menace to society. Rutherford, you are with me?

RUTH. By God! I am!

IS. You're mad!

PLIM. You don't agree with me?

IS. It's not to be thought of! You're forgetting yourself, Plimpton...

PLIM. [Gazing about.] This is no place to discuss it. But I tell you that if there is no support from London...

RUTH. [Starting.] Come... perhaps there may be word! [They start left.] We may beat them yet... who can tell?

[PLIMPTON, RUTHERFORD and ISMAN go off.]

HAGEN. [Emerges with GERALD from shadows, shaking with laughter.] Hat ha! ha! Love and self-sacrifice! You see, Gerald!

GER. Yes... I see! [Looks right... then starts violently.] My sister!

HAGEN. Ah!

GER. What does this mean?

HAGEN. [To ESTELLE, who enters, right, evidently agitated.] Miss Isman!

EST. My father said...

HAGEN. Yes. Won't you sit down?

EST. [Hesitatingly.] Why... I suppose so...

HAGEN. [To GERALD.] Will you excuse us, please, Gerald?

GER. [Amazed.] Why, yes... but Estelle...

EST. [In a faint voice.] Please go, Gerald.

GER. Oh! very well. [Exit, left.]

EST. You wished to see me.

HAGEN. Yes. [Sitting opposite.] How do you like it all?

EST. It is very beautiful.

HAGEN. Do you really think so?

EST. [Wondering.] Don't you?

HAGEN. No.

EST. Truly?

HAGEN. No.

EST. Then why did you do it?

HAGEN. To please you.

EST. [Shrinks.] Oh!

HAGEN. [Fixes his gaze on her, and slowly leans across table; with intensity.] Haven't you discovered yet that you are mine?

EST. [Half rising.] Prince Hagen!

HAGEN. How long will it be before you know it?

EST. How dare you?

HAGEN. Listen. I am a man accustomed to command. I have no time to play with conventions... I cannot dally and plead. But I love you. I cannot live without you! And I will shake the foundations of the world to get you!

EST. [Staring, fascinated; whispers.] Prince Hagen!

HAGEN. All this... [waving his hand] I did in the hope that it would bring you here... so that I might have a chance to tell you. Simply for that one purpose. I have broken the business world to my will... that also was to make you mine!

EST. [Wildly.] You have ruined my father!

HAGEN. Your father has played this game, and his path is strewn with the rivals he has ruined. He knows that, and you know it. Now I have played the game; and I have beaten him. It took me one day to bring him down... [Laughs.] It will take me less time to put him back again.

EST. But why, why?

HAGEN. Listen, Estelle. I came to this civilization of yours, and looked at it. It seemed to me that it was built upon knavery and fraud ... that it was altogether a vile thing... rotten to the core of it! And I said I would smash it, as a child smashes a toy; I would toss it about... as your brother the poet tosses his metaphors. But then I saw you, and in a flash all that was changed. You were beautiful... you were interesting. You were something in the world worth winning... something I had not known about before. But you stood upon the pinnacle of Privilege... you gathered the clouds about your head. How should I climb to you?

EST. [Frightened.] I see!

HAGEN. I came to your home... I was turned from the door. So I set to work to break my way to you.

EST. I see!

HAGEN. And that is how I love you. You are all there is in the game to me. I bring the world and lay it at your feet. It is all yours. You do not like what I do with it, perhaps. Very well... take it and do better. The power is yours for the asking! Power without end! [He reaches out his arms to her; a pause.] You do not like my way of love-making, perhaps. You find me harsh and rude. But I love you. And where, among the men that you know, will you find one who can feel for you what I feel... who would dare for you what I have dared? [Gazes at her with intensity.] Take your time. I have no wish to hurry you. But you must know that, wherever you go, my hand is upon you. All that I do, I do for the love of you.

EST. [Weakly.] I... you frighten me!

HAGEN. All the world I lay at your feet! You shall see.

PLIM. [Off left.] Prince Hagen!

HAGEN. [Starting.] Ah!

PLIM. [Enters, running, in great agitation, with a telegram.] Prince Hagen!

HAGEN. Well?

PLIM. I have a report from London. The market has gone all to pieces!

HAGEN. Ah!

PLIM. Pennsylvania coal is down twenty-five points in the first half hour. I'm lost... everything is lost!

RUTH. [Running on.] Prince Hagen! Steel is down to four! And the Bank of England suspends payments! What...

PLIM. What do you want with us? What are you trying to do?

RUTH. [Wildly.] You've crushed us! We're helpless, utterly helpless!

PLIM. Have you no mercy? Aren't you satisfied when you've got us down?

RUTH. Are you going to ruin everybody? Are you a madman?

PLIM. What are you trying to do? What do you want?

HAGEN. [Has been listening in silence. Suddenly he leaps into action, an expression of furious rage coming upon his face. His eyes gleam, and he raises his hand as if to strike the two.] Get down on your knees!

PLIM. Ha!

RUTH. What?

HAGEN. [Louder.] Get down on your knees! [PLIMPTON sinks in horror. PRINCE HAGEN turns Upon RUTHERFORD.] Down!

RUTH. [Sinking.] Mercy!

HAGEN. [As they kneel before him, his anger vanishes; he steps back.] There! [Waving his hand.] You asked me what I wanted? I wanted this. .. to see you there... upon your knees! [To spectators, who appear right and left.] Behold!

RUTH. Oh! [Starts to rise.]

HAGEN. [Savagely.] Stay where you are!... To see you on your knees! To hear you crying for mercy, which you will not get! You pious plunderers! Devourers of the people! Assassins of women and helpless children! Who made the rules of this game... you or I? Who cast the halo of righteousness about it... who sanctified it by the laws of God and man? Property! Property was holy! Property must rule! You carved it into your constitutions... you taught it in your newspapers, you preached it from your pulpits! You screwed down wages, you screwed up prices... it must be right, because it paid! Money was the test... money was the end! You were business men! Practical men! Don't you know the phrases? Money talks! Business is business! The gold standard... ha, ha, ha! The gold standard! Now someone has come who has more gold than you. You were masters... now I am the master! And what you have done to the people I will do to you! You shall drink the cup that you have poured out for them... you shall drink it to the dregs!

PLIM. [Starting to rise.] Monster!

HAGEN. Stay where you are! Cringe and grovel and whine! [Draws a Nibelung whip from under his coat.] I will put the lash upon your backs! I will strip your shams from you... I will see you as you are! I will take away your wealth, that you have wrung from others! Before I get through with you you shall sweat with the toilers in the trenches! For I am the master now! I have the gold! I own the property! The world is mine! You were lords and barons... you ruled in your little principalities! But I shall rule everywhere... everything... all civilization! I shall be king! King! [With exultant gesture.] Make way for the king! Make way for the king!

CURTAIN

ACT IV

[The scene shows a spacious room, fitted with luxurious rusticity. To the right of centre are a couple of broad windows, leading to a veranda. In the corner, right is a table, with a telephone. In the centre of the room is a large table, with a lamp and books, and a leather arm-chair at each side. To the left of centre is a spacious stone fireplace, having within it a trap door opening downward. At the left a piano with a violin upon it. There are exposed oak beams; antlers, rifles, snowshoes, etc., upon the walls. Entrances right and left.]

[At rise: CALKINS, standing by the desk, arranging some papers.]

CALKINS. [As 'phone rings.] Hello! Yes, this is the Isman camp. Prince Hagen is staying here. This is his secretary speaking. No, Prince Hagen does not receive telephone calls. No, not under any circumstances whatever. It doesn't make any difference. If the President of the United States has anything to say to Prince Hagen, let him communicate with Mr. Isman at his New York office, and the message will reach him. I am sorry... those are my instructions. Good-bye. [To HICKS, who enters with telegram.] Hicks, for the future, Prince Hagen wishes all messages for him to be taken to my office. That applies to letters, telegrams... everything.

HICKS. Very good, sir. [Exit.]

CAL. [Opening a telegram.] More appeals for mercy.

HAGEN. [Enters from veranda, wearing white flannels, cool and alert.] Well, Calkins?

CAL. Nothing important, sir.

HAGEN. The market continues to fall?

CAL. Copper is off five points, sir.

HAGEN. Ah!

CAL. The President of the United States tried to get you on the 'phone just now.

HAGEN. Humph! Anything else?

CAL. There has been another mob on Fifth Avenue this morning. They seem to be threatening your palace.

HAGEN. I see. You wrote to the mayor, as I told you?

CAL. Yes, sir.

HAGEN. Well, you'd best put in another hundred guards. And they're to be instructed to shoot.

CAL. Yes, sir.

HAGEN. Let them be men we can depend on... I don't want any mistake about it. I don't care about the building, but I mean to make a test of it.

CAL. I'll see to it, sir.

HAGEN. Anything else?

CAL. A message from a delegation from the National Unemployment Conference. They are to call tomorrow morning.

HAGEN. Ah, yes. Make a note, please... I sympathize with their purpose, and contribute half a million. [To GERALD, who enters, left.] Hello, Gerald... how are you? Make yourself at home. [To CALKINS.] I attribute the present desperate situation to the anarchical struggles of rival financial interests. I am assuming control, and straightening out the tangle as rapidly as I can. The worst of the crisis is over... the opposition is capitulating, and I expect soon to order a general resumption of industry. Prepare me an address of five hundred words... sharp and snappy. Then see the head of the delegation, and have it understood that the affair is not to occupy more than fifteen minutes.

CAL. Very good, sir.

HAGEN. And stir up our Press Bureau. We must have strong, conservative editorials this week... It's the crucial period. Our institutions are at stake... the national honor is imperilled... order must be preserved at any hazard... all that sort of thing.

CAL. Yes, sir... I understand.

HAGEN. Very good. That will be all.

CAL. Yes, sir.

[Exit, right.]

GER. You're putting the screws on, are you?

HAGEN. Humph! Yes. It's funny to hear these financial men... their one idea in life has been to dominate... and now they cry out against tyranny!

GER. I can imagine it.

HAGEN. Here's Plimpton, making speeches about American democracy! These fellows have got so used to making pretenses that they actually deceive themselves.

GER. I've noticed that you make a few yourself now.

HAGEN. Yes... don't I do it well? [Thoughtfully.] You know, Gerald, pretenses are the greatest device that your civilization had to teach me.

GER. Indeed?

HAGEN. We never made any pretenses in Nibelheim; and when I first met you, your talk about virtue and morality and self-sacrifice was simply incomprehensible to me. It seemed something quite apart from life. But now I've come to perceive that this is what makes possible the system under which you live.

GER. Explain yourself.

HAGEN. Here is this civilization... simply appalling in its vastness. The countless millions of your people, the wealth you have piled up... it seems like a huge bubble that may burst any minute. And the one device by which it is all kept together... is pretense!

GER. Why do you think that?

HAGEN. Life, Gerald, is the survival of the strong. I care not if it be in a jungle or in a city, it is the warfare of each against all. But in the former case it's brute force, and in the latter it's power of mind. And don't you see that the ingenious device which makes the animal of the slums the docile slave of the man who can outwit him.. . is this Morality... this absolutely sublimest invention, this most daring conception that ever flashed across the mind of man?

GER. Oh, I see.

HAGEN. I used to wonder at it down there on the Bowery. The poor are a thousand to your one, and the best that is might be theirs, if they chose to take it; but there is Morality! They call it their virtue. And so the rich man may have his vices in peace. By heaven, if that is not a wondrous achievement, I have not seen one!

GER. You believe this morality was invented by the rich.

HAGEN. I don't know. It seems to be a congenital disease.

GER. Some people believe it was implanted in man by God.

HAGEN. [Shrugging his shoulders.] Perhaps. Or by a devil. Men might have lived in holes, like woodchucks, and been fat and happy; but now they have Morality, and toil and die for some other man's delight.

CAL. [Enters, right.] Are you at leisure, sir?

HAGEN. Why?

CAL. Mr. Isman wants you on the 'phone.

HAGEN. Oh! All right... [Goes to 'phone.]

GER. [Rises.] Perhaps I...

HAGEN. No, that's all right. [Sits at 'phone.] Hello! Is that Isman? How are you? [To CALKINS.] Calkins!

CAL. Yes, sir.

[Sits and takes notes.]

HAGEN. How about Intercontinental? [Imperiously.] But I can! I said the stock was to go to sixty-four, and I want it to go. I don't care what

it costs, Isman... let it go in the morning... and don't ever let this
happen again. I have sent word you are to have another hundred million
by nine-thirty. Will that do? Don't take chances. Oh, Rutherford!
Tell Rutherford my terms are that the directors of the Fidelity Life
Insurance Company are to resign, and he is to go to China for six
months. Yes. I mean that literally... Plimpton? What do I want with his
banks... I've got my own money... And, oh, by the way, Isman... call up
the White House again, and tell the President that the regulars will
be needed in New York.... No, I understand you... I think I've fixed
matters up at this end. I've got two hundred guards up here, and they're
picked men... they'll shoot if there's need. I'm not talking about it,
naturally... but I'm taking care of myself. You keep your nerve, Isman.
It'll all be over in a month or two more... these fellows are used to
having their own way, and they make a fuss. And, by the way, as to the
newspapers... we'll turn out that paper trust crowd, and stop selling
paper to the ones that are making trouble. That'll put an end to it,
I fancy. You had best get after it yourself, and have it attended to
promptly. You might think of little things like that yourself, Isman...
no, you're all right; only you haven't got enough imagination. But
just get onto this job, and let me hear that it's done before morning.
Good-bye. [Hangs up receiver.] Humph! [To GERALD.] They've about got
your father's nerve.

GER. I can't say that I blame him very much. [In somber thought.]
Really, you know, Prince Hagen, this can't go on. What's to be the end
of it?

HAGEN. [Laughing.] Oh, come, come, Gerald... don't bother your head with
things like that! You're a poet... you must keep your imagination free
from such dismal matters.... See, I've got a job for you. [Pointing to
books on table.] Do you notice the titles?

GER. [Has been handling the books absent-mindedly; now looks at titles.]

The Saints' Everlasting Rest. Pilgrim's Progress. The Life of St. Ignatius.... What does that mean?

HAGEN. I'm studying up on religion. I want to know the language.

GER. I See!

HAGEN. But I don't seem to get hold of it very well. I think it's the job for you.

GER. How do you mean?

HAGEN. I'm getting ready to introduce Morality into Nibelheim.

GER. What?

HAGEN. [Playfully.] You remember you talked to me about it a long time ago. And now I've come to your way of thinking. Suppose I gave you a chance to civilize the place, to teach those wretched creatures to love beauty and virtue?

GER. It would depend upon what your motive was in inviting me.

HAGEN. My Motive? What has that to do with it? Virtue is virtue, is it not?... No matter what I think about it?

GER. Yes.

HAGEN. And virtue is its own reward?

GER. Perhaps so.

HAGEN. Let us grant that the consequences of educating and elevating the Nibelungs... of teaching them to love righteousness... would be that they were deprived of all their gold, and forced to labor at getting more for a wicked capitalist like me. Would it not still be right to teach them?

GER. It might, perhaps.

HAGEN. Then you will try it?

GER. No... I'm afraid not.

HAGEN. Why not?

GER. [Gravely.] Well... for one thing... I have weighty reasons for doubting the perfectibility of the Nibelungs.

HAGEN. [Gazes at him; then shakes with laughter.] Really, Gerald, that is the one clever thing I've heard you say!

GER. [Laughing.] Thank you!

HAGEN. [Rises and looks at watch.] Your mother was coming down. Ah! Mrs. Isman!

MRS. IS. [Enters, left.] Good afternoon, Prince Hagen.

HAGEN. And how go things?

MRS. IS. I've just had a telegram from my brother. He says that the Archbishop of Canterbury never goes abroad, and was shocked at the suggestion; but he thinks two million might fetch him.

HAGEN. Very well... offer it.

MRS. IS. Do you really think it's worth that?

HAGEN. My dear lady, it is worth anything if it will make you happy and add to the eclat of the wedding. There's nothing too good for Estelle.

MRS. IS. Ah, what a wonderful man you are. [Eyeing him.] I was wondering how rose pink would go with your complexion.

HAGEN. Dear me! Am I to wear rose pink?

MRS. IS. No, but I'm planning the decoration for the wedding breakfast .... And I'm puzzled about the flowers. I'm weary of orchids and la France roses... Mrs. Bagley-Willis had her ball room swamped with them last week.

HAGEN. We must certainly not imitate Mrs. Bagley-Willis.

MRS. IS. [Complacently.] I fancy she's pretty nearly at the end of her rope. My maid tells me she couldn't pay her grocer's bill till she got that million from you!

HAGEN. Ha, ha, ha!

MRS. IS. I wish you'd come with me for a moment... I have some designs for the breakfast menu...

HAGEN. Delighted, I'm sure. [They go off, left.]

GER. Oh, my God!

EST. [Enters in a beautiful afternoon gown, and carrying an armful of roses; she is nervous and preoccupied.] Ah! Gerald!

GER. Estelle. [He watches her in silence; she arranges flowers.]

EST. How goes the poem, Gerald?

GER. The poem! Who could think of a poem at a time like this? [Advancing toward her.] Estelle! I can bear it no longer!

EST. What?

GER. This crime! I tell you it's a crime you're committing!

EST. Oh, Gerald! Don't begin that again. You know it's too late. And it tears me to pieces!

GER. I can't help it. I must say it!

EST. [Hurrying toward him.] Brother! You must not say another word to me! I tell you you must not... I can't bear it!

GER. Estelle...

EST. No, I say... no! I've given my word! My honor is pledged, and it's too late to turn back. I have permitted father to incur obligations before all the world.

GER. But, Estelle, you don't know. If you understood all... all...

EST. [With sudden intensity.] Gerald! I know what you mean! I have felt it! You know more about Prince Hagen than you have told me. There is some secret--something strange. [She stares at him wildly.] I don't want to know it! Gerald... don't you understand? We are in that man's hands! We are at his mercy! Don't you know that he would never give me up? He would follow me to the end of the earth! He would wreck the whole world to get me! I am in a cage with a wild beast!

[They stare at each other.]

GER. [In sudden excitement.] Estelle!

EST. What?

GER. Can it be that you love this man?

EST. [Startled.] I don't know! How can I tell? He terrifies me. He fascinates me. I don't know what to make of him. And I don't dare to think. [Wildly.] And what difference does it make? I have promised to marry him!

[MRS. ISMAN enters, left, and listens.]

EST. And I must keep my word! You must not try to dissuade me...

MRS. IS. Estelle!

EST. Mother!

MRS. IS. Has Gerald been tormenting you again? My child, my child.. . I implore you, don't let that madness take hold of you! Think of our position. [Attempts to embrace her.] I know how it is... I went through with it myself. We women all have to go through with it. I did not care for your father... it nearly broke my heart. I was madly in love at the time... truly I was! But think what will become of us...

EST. [Vehemently, pushing her away.] Mother! I forbid you to speak another word to me! I will not bear it! I will keep my bargain. I will do what I have said I will do. But I will not have you talk to me about it... Do you understand me?

MRS. IS. My dear!

EST. Please go! Both of you! I wish to be alone!

MRS. IS. [In great agitation.] Oh, dear me! dear me!

[Exit, left.]

GER. Good-bye!

[Exit, right; ESTELLE recovers herself by an effort; stands by table in thought. Twilight has begun to gather.]

HAGEN. [Enters by veranda.] Ah! Estelle! [Comes toward her.] My beautiful! [Makes to embrace her.] Not yet?

EST. [Faintly.] Prince Hagen, I told you...

HAGEN. I know, I know! But how much longer? I love you! The sight of you is fire in my veins. Have I not been patient? The time is very short... when will you let me...

[Advances.]

EST. [Gasping.] Give me... give me till tomorrow!

HAGEN. [Gripping his hands.] To-morrow! Very well! [Turns to table.] Ah, flowers! Do you like the new poppies?

EST. They are exquisite!

HAGEN. [Sits in chair.] Well, we've had a busy day today.

EST. Yes. You must be tired.

HAGEN. In your house? No!

EST. Rest, even so. [Goes to piano.] I will play for you. [Sits, and takes Rheingold score.] One of Gerald's scores.

[Plays a little, then sounds the Nibelung theme. PRINCE HAGEN starts. She repeats it.]

HAGEN. No... no!

EST. Why-what's the matter?

HAGEN. That music! What is it?

EST. It's some of the Nibelung music. Gerald had it here.

HAGEN. Don't play it! [Hesitating.] Music jars on me now... I've too much on my mind.

EST. [Rising.] Oh... very well. It is time for tea, anyway. Have you talked with father today?

HAGEN. Three times. He is in the thick of the fight. He plays the game well.

EST. He has played it a long time.

HAGEN. Yes. ['Phone rings.] Ah! What is that? [Takes receiver.] Hello!

Yes... oh, Isman! I see' More trouble in Fifth Avenue, hey? Well, are the regulars there? Why don't they fire? Women and children in front! Do they expect to accomplish anything by that? No, don't call me up about matters like that, Isman. The orders have been given. No... not an inch! Let the orders be carried out. That is all. Good-bye. Hangs up receiver.

EST. [Has been listening in terror.] Prince Hagen!

HAGEN. Well?

EST. What does that mean?

HAGEN. It means that the slums are pouring into Fifth Avenue.

EST. [A pause.] What do they want?

HAGEN. Apparently they want to burn my palace.

EST. And the orders... what are the orders?

HAGEN. The orders are to shoot, and to shoot straight.

EST. Is it for me that you are doing this?

HAGEN. How do you mean?

EST. You told me you brought all the world and laid it at my feet. Is this part of the process?

HAGEN. Yes, this is part.

EST. [Stares at him intently; whispers.] How do you do it?

HAGEN. What?

EST. What is the secret of your power? They are millions, and you are
only one... yet you have them bound! Is it some spell that you have
woven? [A pause; HAGEN stares at her. She goes on, with growing
intensity and excitement.] They are afraid of your gold! Afraid of your
gold! All the world is afraid of it! It is nothing--it is a dream ...
it is a nightmare! If they would defy you... if they would open their
eyes... it would go as all nightmares go! But you have made them believe
in it! They cower and cringe before it! They toil and slave for it! They
take up arms and murder their brothers for it! They sell their minds and
their souls for it! And all because no one dares to defy you! No one!
No one! [In a sudden transport of passion.] I defy you! [PRINCE HAGEN
starts; she gazes at him wildly.] I will not marry you! I will not
sell myself to you! Not for any price that you can offer... not for any
threat that you can make! Not in order that my mother may plan wedding
breakfasts and triumph over Mrs. Bagley-Willis! Not in order that my
father may rule in Wall Street and command the slaughter of women and
children! Nor yet for the fear of anything that you can do!

HAGEN. [In a low voice.] Have you any idea what I will do?

EST. [Desperately.] I know what you mean... you have me at your mercy!
You have your guards--I am in a trap! And you mean force... I have felt
it in all your actions... behind all your words. Very well! There is a
way of escape, even from that; and I will take it! You can compel me to
kill myself; but you can never compel me to marry you! Not with all the
power you can summon... not with all the wealth of the world! Do you
understand me? [They stare at each other.] I have heard you talk with my
brother, and I know what are your ideas. You came to our civilization,
and tried it, and found it a lie. Virtue and honor... justice and
mercy... all these things were pretenses... snares for the unwary. There

was no one you could not frighten with your gold! That is your creed,
and so far it has served you... but no farther! There is one thing in
the world you cannot get... one thing that is beyond the reach of all
your cunning! And that is a woman's soul. [With a gesture of exultant
triumph.] You cannot buy me!

HAGEN. Estelle!

EST. Go!

HAGEN. [Stretching out his arms to her.] I love you!

EST. You love me! The slave driver... with his golden whip!

HAGEN. Even so... I love you.

EST. What do you know of love? What does the word mean to you?
Before love must come justice and honor, with it come mercy and
self-sacrifice... all things that you deride and trample on. What have
you to do with love?

HAGEN. [With intensity.] I love you! More than anything else in all the
world... I love you!

EST. [Stares at him.] More than your power?

HAGEN. Estelle! Listen to me! You do not know what my life has been! But
I can say this for myself... I have sought the best that I know. I have
sought Reality. [A pause.] I seek your love! I seek those things which
you have, and which I have not. [Fiercely.] Do you think that I have not
felt the difference?

EST. [In a startled whisper.] No!

HAGEN. That which you have, and which I have not, has become all the world to me! I love you... I cannot live without you. I will follow you wherever you command. Only teach me how to win your love.

EST. I cannot make terms with you. I will not hear of love from you while you have force in your hands.

HAGEN. I will leave your home. I will set you free. I will humble myself before you. What else can I do?

EST. You can lay down your power.

HAGEN. Estelle! Those are mere words.

EST. No!

HAGEN. Who is to take up the power? Shall I hand it back to those who had it before? Are Plimpton and Rutherford better fitted to wield it than I?

EST. [Vehemently.] Give it to the people!

HAGEN. The people! Do you believe that in that mass of ignorance and corruption which you call the people there is the power to rule the world?

EST. What is it that has made the people corrupt? What is it that has kept them in ignorance? What is it but your gold? It lies upon them like a mountain's weight! It crushes every aspiration for freedom... every effort after light! Teach them... help them... then see if they cannot govern themselves!

HAGEN. I meant to do it...

EST. Yes... so does every rich man! When only he has the time to think of it! When only his power is secure! I have heard my father say it... a score of times. But there are always new rivals to trample... new foes to fight... new wrongs and horrors to be perpetrated! The time to do it is now... NOW!

HAGEN. Estelle...

CAL. [Enters hurriedly.] Prince Hagen!

HAGEN. What is it?

CAL. A message from Isman. There is bad news from Washington.

HAGEN. Well?

CAL. A. bill has been introduced in Congress... it is expected to pass both houses to-night... your property is to be confiscated!

HAGEN. What!

CAL. The sources of natural wealth... the land and the mines and the railroads... all are to become public property. It is to take effect at once!

EST. [Pointing at him in exultation.] Aha! It has come!

[They stare at each other.]

CAL. I tried to get more information... but I was cut off...

HAGEN. Cut off!

CAL. I think the wires are down... I can't get any response.

HAGEN. I see! [Stands in deep thought; laughs.] Well... [To ESTELLE.] At least Plimpton and Rutherford are buried with me! [To CALKINS.] Send to town at once and have the wires seen to. And try to learn what you can.

CAL. Yes, sir... at once! [Exit.]

EST. They have done it themselves, you see!

HAGEN. Yes... I see.

GER. [Enters, centre; stands looking from one to the other.] Well, Prince Hagen... it looks as if the game was up.

HAGEN. You've heard the news?

GER. From Washington? Yes. And more than that. Your guards have revolted.

HAGEN. What! Here?

GER. Yes. We're prisoners of war, it seems.

EST. Gerald!

HAGEN. How do you know?

GER. They've sent a delegation to tell us. They've cut the telephone wires, blocked the roads, and shut us in.

HAGEN. What do they want?

GER. They don't condescend to tell us that. They simply inform us that the woods are guarded, and that anyone who tries to leave the camp will be shot.

EST. [In fright.] Prince Hagen!

[HAGEN stands motionless.]

GER. [Solemnly.] Hagen, the game is up!

HAGEN. [In deep thought.] Yes. The game is up. [A pause.] Gerald!

GER. Well?

HAGEN. [Points to violin.] Play!

GER. [Startled.] No!

HAGEN. Play!

GER. You will go?

HAGEN. Yes. I will go. But I will come back! Play! [GERALD takes the violin and plays the Nibelung theme.] Louder!

GERALD plays the Nibelung music, which is taken up by the orchestra and mounts to a climax, in the midst of which HAGEN pronounces a sort of incantation.

Mimi! Mimi! Open the gates of wonderland! Bring back the mood of phantasy, and wake us from our evil dream!

Silence. Then answering echoes of the music are heard, faintly, from the fireplace. There are rappings and murmurings underground, rumbling and patter of feet, and all the sounds of Nibelheim. As the music swells louder, the trap doors slide open, and MIMI appears, amid steam and glare of light. ESTELLE sees him, and recoils in terror. A company of Nibelungs emerge one by one. They peer about timidly, recognize HAGEN, and with much trepidation approach him. MIMI clasps his hand, and they surround him with joyful cries. He moves toward the fireplace, and the steam envelops him.

EST. [Starts toward him, stretching out her arms to him.] Prince Hagen!

HAGEN. Farewell!

He gradually retires, and disappears with the Nibelungs. The orchestra sounds the motive of Siegfried Triumphant.

CURTAIN

The Codes Of Hammurabi And Moses
W. W. Davies

QTY

The discovery of the Hammurabi Code is one of the greatest achievements of archaeology, and is of paramount interest, not only to the student of the Bible, but also to all those interested in ancient history...

Religion   **ISBN: *1-59462-338-4***   **Pages:132**
MSRP $12.95

The Theory of Moral Sentiments
Adam Smith

QTY

This work from 1749. contains original theories of conscience amd moral judgment and it is the foundation for systemof morals.

Philosophy ISBN: *1-59462-777-0*   **Pages:536**
MSRP $19.95

Jessica's First Prayer
Hesba Stretton

QTY

In a screened and secluded corner of one of the many railway-bridges which span the streets of London there could be seen a few years ago, from five o'clock every morning until half past eight, a tidily set-out coffee-stall, consisting of a trestle and board, upon which stood two large tin cans, with a small fire of charcoal burning under each so as to keep the coffee boiling during the early hours of the morning when the work-people were thronging into the city on their way to their daily toil...

Pages:84

Childrens   ISBN: *1-59462-373-2*   *MSRP $9.95*

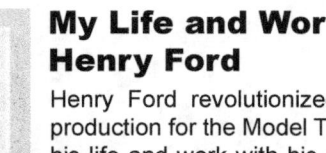

My Life and Work
Henry Ford

QTY

Henry Ford revolutionized the world with his implementation of mass production for the Model T automobile. Gain valuable business insight into his life and work with his own auto-biography... "We have only started on our development of our country we have not as yet, with all our talk of wonderful progress, done more than scratch the surface. The progress has been wonderful enough but..."

Pages:300

Biographies/   ISBN: *1-59462-198-5*   *MSRP $21.95*

The Art of Cross-Examination
Francis Wellman

QTY

I presume it is the experience of every author, after his first book is published upon an important subject, to be almost overwhelmed with a wealth of ideas and illustrations which could readily have been included in his book, and which to his own mind, at least, seem to make a second edition inevitable. Such certainly was the case with me; and when the first edition had reached its sixth impression in five months, I rejoiced to learn that it seemed to my publishers that the book had met with a sufficiently favorable reception to justify a second and considerably enlarged edition. ...

Pages:412

Reference   ISBN: *1-59462-647-2*   *MSRP $19.95*

On the Duty of Civil Disobedience
Henry David Thoreau

QTY

Thoreau wrote his famous essay, On the Duty of Civil Disobedience, as a protest against an unjust but popular war and the immoral but popular institution of slave-owning. He did more than write—he declined to pay his taxes, and was hauled off to gaol in consequence. Who can say how much this refusal of his hastened the end of the war and of slavery ?

Law   ISBN: *1-59462-747-9*

Pages:48

MSRP $7.45

Dream Psychology Psychoanalysis for Beginners
Sigmund Freud

QTY

Sigmund Freud, born Sigismund Schlomo Freud (May 6, 1856 - September 23, 1939), was a Jewish-Austrian neurologist and psychiatrist who co-founded the psychoanalytic school of psychology. Freud is best known for his theories of the unconscious mind, especially involving the mechanism of repression; his redefinition of sexual desire as mobile and directed towards a wide variety of objects; and his therapeutic techniques, especially his understanding of transference in the therapeutic relationship and the presumed value of dreams as sources of insight into unconscious desires.

Pages:196

Psychology   ISBN: *1-59462-905-6*   *MSRP $15.45*

The Miracle of Right Thought
Orison Swett Marden

QTY

Believe with all of your heart that you will do what you were made to do. When the mind has once formed the habit of holding cheerful, happy, prosperous pictures, it will not be easy to form the opposite habit. It does not matter how improbable or how far away this realization may see, or how dark the prospects may be, if we visualize them as best we can, as vividly as possible, hold tenaciously to them and vigorously struggle to attain them, they will gradually become actualized, realized in the life. But a desire, a longing without endeavor, a yearning abandoned or held indifferently will vanish without realization.

Pages:360

Self Help   ISBN: *1-59462-644-8*   *MSRP $25.45*

QTY

The Rosicrucian Cosmo-Conception Mystic Christianity *by Max Heindel*　ISBN: *1-59462-188-8*　**$38.95**
The Rosicrucian Cosmo-conception is not dogmatic, neither does it appeal to any other authority than the reason of the student. It is: not controversial, but is: sent forth in the, hope that it may help to clear...　New Age/Religion Pages 646

Abandonment To Divine Providence *by Jean-Pierre de Caussade*　ISBN: *1-59462-228-0*　**$25.95**
"The Rev. Jean Pierre de Caussade was one of the most remarkable spiritual writers of the Society of Jesus in France in the 18th Century. His death took place at Toulouse in 1751. His works have gone through many editions and have been republished...　Inspirational/Religion Pages 400

Mental Chemistry *by Charles Haanel*　ISBN: *1-59462-192-6*　**$23.95**
Mental Chemistry allows the change of material conditions by combining and appropriately utilizing the power of the mind. Much like applied chemistry creates something new and unique out of careful combinations of chemicals the mastery of mental chemistry...　New Age Pages 354

The Letters of Robert Browning and Elizabeth Barret Barrett 1845-1846 vol II　ISBN: *1-59462-193-4*　**$35.95**
by Robert Browning and Elizabeth Barrett　Biographies Pages 596

Gleanings In Genesis (volume I) *by Arthur W. Pink*　ISBN: *1-59462-130-6*　**$27.45**
Appropriately has Genesis been termed "the seed plot of the Bible" for in it we have, in germ form, almost all of the great doctrines which are afterwards fully developed in the books of Scripture which follow...　Religion/Inspirational Pages 420

The Master Key *by L. W. de Laurence*　ISBN: *1-59462-001-6*　**$30.95**
In no branch of human knowledge has there been a more lively increase of the spirit of research during the past few years than in the study of Psychology, Concentration and Mental Discipline. The requests for authentic lessons in Thought Control, Mental Discipline and...　New Age/Business Pages 422

The Lesser Key Of Solomon Goetia *by L. W. de Laurence*　ISBN: *1-59462-092-X*　**$9.95**
This translation of the first book of the "Lernegton" which is now for the first time made accessible to students of Talismanic Magic was done, after careful collation and edition, from numerous Ancient Manuscripts in Hebrew, Latin, and French...　New Age/Occult Pages 92

Rubaiyat Of Omar Khayyam *by Edward Fitzgerald*　ISBN:*1-59462-332-5*　**$13.95**
Edward Fitzgerald, whom the world has already learned, in spite of his own efforts to remain within the shadow of anonymity, to look upon as one of the rarest poets of the century, was born at Bredfield, in Suffolk, on the 31st of March, 1809. He was the third son of John Purcell...　Music Pages 172

Ancient Law *by Henry Maine*　ISBN: *1-59462-128-4*　**$29.95**
The chief object of the following pages is to indicate some of the earliest ideas of mankind, as they are reflected in Ancient Law, and to point out the relation of those ideas to modern thought.　Religiom/History Pages 452

Far-Away Stories *by William J. Locke*　ISBN: *1-59462-129-2*　**$19.45**
"Good wine needs no bush, but a collection of mixed vintages does. And this book is just such a collection. Some of the stories I do not want to remain buried for ever in the museum files of dead magazine-numbers an author's not unpardonable vanity..."　Fiction Pages 272

Life of David Crockett *by David Crockett*　ISBN: *1-59462-250-7*　**$27.45**
"Colonel David Crockett was one of the most remarkable men of the times in which he lived. Born in humble life, but gifted with a strong will, an indomitable courage, and unremitting perseverance...　Biographies/New Age Pages 424

Lip-Reading *by Edward Nitchie*　ISBN: *1-59462-206-X*　**$25.95**
Edward B. Nitchie, founder of the New York School for the Hard of Hearing, now the Nitchie School of Lip-Reading, Inc, wrote "LIP-READING Principles and Practice". The development and perfecting of this meritorious work on lip-reading was an undertaking...　How-to Pages 400

A Handbook of Suggestive Therapeutics, Applied Hypnotism, Psychic Science　ISBN: *1-59462-214-0*　**$24.95**
by Henry Munro　Health/New Age/Health/Self-help Pages 376

A Doll's House: and Two Other Plays *by Henrik Ibsen*　ISBN: *1-59462-112-8*　**$19.95**
Henrik Ibsen created this classic when in revolutionary 1848 Rome. Introducing some striking concepts in playwriting for the realist genre, this play has been studied the world over.　Fiction/Classics/Plays 308

The Light of Asia *by sir Edwin Arnold*　ISBN: *1-59462-204-3*　**$13.95**
In this poetic masterpiece, Edwin Arnold describes the life and teachings of Buddha. The man who was to become known as Buddha to the world was born as Prince Gautama of India but he rejected the worldly riches and abandoned the reigns of power when...　Religion/History/Biographies Pages 170

The Complete Works of Guy de Maupassant *by Guy de Maupassant*　ISBN: *1-59462-157-8*　**$16.95**
"For days and days, nights and nights, I had dreamed of that first kiss which was to consecrate our engagement, and I knew not on what spot I should put my lips..."　Fiction/Classics Pages 240

The Art of Cross-Examination *by Francis L. Wellman*　ISBN: *1-59462-309-0*　**$26.95**
Written by a renowned trial lawyer, Wellman imparts his experience and uses case studies to explain how to use psychology to extract desired information through questioning.　How-to/Science/Reference Pages 408

Answered or Unanswered? *by Louisa Vaughan*　ISBN: *1-59462-248-5*　**$10.95**
Miracles of Faith in China　Religion Pages 112

The Edinburgh Lectures on Mental Science (1909) *by Thomas*　ISBN: *1-59462-008-3*　**$11.95**
This book contains the substance of a course of lectures recently given by the writer in the Queen Street Hail, Edinburgh. Its purpose is to indicate the Natural Principles governing the relation between Mental Action and Material Conditions...　New Age/Psychology Pages 148

Ayesha *by H. Rider Haggard*　ISBN: *1-59462-301-5*　**$24.95**
Verily and indeed it is the unexpected that happens! Probably if there was one person upon the earth from whom the Editor of this, and of a certain previous history, did not expect to hear again...　Classics Pages 380

Ayala's Angel *by Anthony Trollope*　ISBN: *1-59462-352-X*　**$29.95**
The two girls were both pretty, but Lucy who was twenty-one who supposed to be simple and comparatively unattractive, whereas Ayala was credited, as her Bombwhat romantic name might show, with poetic charm and a taste for romance. Ayala when her father died was nineteen...　Fiction Pages 484

The American Commonwealth *by James Bryce*　ISBN: *1-59462-286-8*　**$34.45**
An interpretation of American democratic political theory. It examines political mechanics and society from the perspective of Scotsman James Bryce　Politics Pages 572

Stories of the Pilgrims *by Margaret P. Pumphrey*　ISBN: *1-59462-116-0*　**$17.95**
This book explores pilgrims religious oppression in England as well as their escape to Holland and eventual crossing to America on the Mayflower, and their early days in New England...　History Pages 268

QTY

The Fasting Cure by *Sinclair Upton*   ISBN: *1-59462-222-1* **$13.95**
In the Cosmopolitan Magazine for May, 1910, and in the Contemporary Review (London) for April, 1910, I published an article dealing with my experiences in fasting. I have written a great many magazine articles, but never one which attracted so much attention... New Age/Self Help/Health Pages 164

Hebrew Astrology by *Sepharial*   ISBN: *1-59462-308-2* **$13.45**
In these days of advanced thinking it is a matter of common observation that we have left many of the old landmarks behind and that we are now pressing forward to greater heights and to a wider horizon than that which represented the mind-content of our progenitors... Astrology Pages 144

Thought Vibration or The Law of Attraction in the Thought World   ISBN: *1-59462-127-6* **$12.95**
by *William Walker Atkinson*   Psychology/Religion Pages 144

Optimism by *Helen Keller*   ISBN: *1-59462-108-X* **$15.95**
Helen Keller was blind, deaf, and mute since 19 months old, yet famously learned how to overcome these handicaps, communicate with the world, and spread her lectures promoting optimism. An inspiring read for everyone... Biographies/Inspirational Pages 84

Sara Crewe by *Frances Burnett*   ISBN: *1-59462-360-0* **$9.45**
In the first place, Miss Minchin lived in London. Her home was a large, dull, tall one, in a large, dull square, where all the houses were alike, and all the sparrows were alike, and where all the door-knockers made the same heavy sound... Childrens/Classic Pages 88

The Autobiography of Benjamin Franklin by *Benjamin Franklin*   ISBN: *1-59462-135-7* **$24.95**
The Autobiography of Benjamin Franklin has probably been more extensively read than any other American historical work, and no other book of its kind has had such ups and downs of fortune. Franklin lived for many years in England, where he was agent... Biographies/History Pages 332

Name	
Email	
Telephone	
Address	
City, State ZIP	

☐ **Credit Card**   ☐ **Check / Money Order**

Credit Card Number	
Expiration Date	
Signature	

Please Mail to: Book Jungle
PO Box 2226
Champaign, IL 61825
or Fax to: 630-214-0564

ORDERING INFORMATION
web: *www.bookjungle.com*
email: *sales@bookjungle.com*
fax: *630-214-0564*
mail: *Book Jungle PO Box 2226 Champaign, IL 61825*
or PayPal *to sales@bookjungle.com*

Please contact us for bulk discounts

DIRECT-ORDER TERMS
**20% Discount if You Order
Two or More Books**
Free Domestic Shipping!
Accepted: Master Card, Visa,
Discover, American Express

www.ingramcontent.com/pod-product-compliance
Lightning Source LLC
Chambersburg PA
CBHW082014170626
46817CB00009B/3097